The

DuBois

Curse

JJV: The Storyteller

JJV: The Storyteller Presents
The Dubois Curse

Copyright © 2015 by JJV

ISBN-13: 978-0692460856 (Custom Universal)
ISBN-10: 0692460853
LCCN: 2015942974
Editing: Twenty-First Street Urban Editing / Jill Alicea
Typesetting: Twenty-First Street Urban Editing

Acknowledgments

A BIG thank you to all who supported me with my first book, *Can't Nobody*. I must send a special acknowledgement to my mother, Barbara, and my brother, Marcus, who both have been extremely supportive of me with my new chosen career. And a big shout-out to my editor and the staff at 21st Street Urban Editing - you are da bomb!

Thank you family, and friends that I have also chosen as family. There are too many of you to name, but know that you have been an important part of my success. Thank you to my new readers. I trust that this second book will not let you down.

And last, but never least, thank you Lord for being the conductor of my life. Without You, none of this would be possible.

Dedications

This book is dedicated to my two sons, Justin and Bryson. I love you both with all of my heart and soul. I may have not always made the right decisions, but I have always loved you. There is no love greater than the love of a mother for her children, demonstrated by the love of God for us.

I also want to dedicate this book to all of the young mothers out there raising their children on their own. Remember, you are never alone if you have God with you. You can do all things though Christ who strengthens you. And in the words of the prophetic Tupac, "Keep Your Head Up."

Lastly, this book is dedicated to my mother, who spent many of nights praying and supporting me through my life's journey. I know it has not always been easy, but thanks for hanging in there. I love you!

Chapter 1

My name is Mystery DuBois and I come from a long line of hos. They say that I am a ho, my mother was a ho, and my grandmother was a ho. I call it the DuBois Curse. All the DuBois women had only one daughter. We all had an exotic look about us that made us look as if we were probably a mix of Asian and Black. As far as I knew, we were as black as everyone else in the Ward. But because we had a different look, we often stood out and attracted a lot of men while many women were not very fond of us.

My daughter was also very beautiful, but I'll be damned if my daughter will be a ho like the DuBois women that came before her. My grandmother owned a ho house and was considered the Madam of 3rd Ward. My grandmother always said that although my mom was an accident, she was also a financial blessing, so she decided to name my mother Prosperity. My grandmother pimped my mom out to men at a very early age. My mother knew nothing other than ho'in'. My mom told me she named me Mystery because it was a damn mystery to her who my father was.

Unlike my mother, I knew exactly who my baby's daddy was. I was raped by one of the big drug dealers in the hood and had my daughter when I was eleven years old. He came by to see my mom and since she was not there, he said I would do. When I told her what happened, she told me it was my fault because I should not have opened the door for him. I can't say my mother abused me like her mother did her, but she sure in the hell never took care of me. She left me to fend for myself.

Once my stomach began getting big, my mother forced me to stop going to school. She said that if CPS found out I was pregnant, she would go to jail and I would go to foster care. I knew kids in foster care and I did not want that. I stayed confined to the house for six months. No one cared that I had dropped out of school. They assumed that I was just ho'in' like the rest of my family.

We delivered my daughter Porchia at the house with the help of Aunt Hattie. My mom told me that we had to keep Porchia a secret. After Porchia was born, I only left the house to run errands for my mom. She reminded me every time I stepped out not to mention Porchia to anyone. I did not know anything about being a mother, nor did my mother. But the one thing I knew was that I wanted to try to be a good mother to my daughter. My mission was to make sure, at any cost, that my daughter did not grow up to be a ho.

My mom died in her bedroom from an overdose from shooting up heroin shortly after I gave birth to

Porchia. I did not tell anyone until four days later because no one was supposed to know about Porchia. One day my mom's pimp, Lenny, insisted on pushing his way into the house. He went crazy, asking me what happened. I told him that my mom had died from an overdose of drugs and I was afraid to tell anyone because I did not want them to take me and my sister, Porchia, away. Lenny did not know what to do so he called my grandmother's good friend and her ex-bottom ho, Hattie Mae Williams. Aunt Hattie, as I called her, always knew how to fix any problem.

Aunt Hattie used to be the rawest bottom ho around. She took no mess from anyone. Aunt Hattie was a big, red-boned woman who everyone said was mean because she had Indian blood in her. She was a few years younger than my grandmother but she knew how to handle all of the hos and she brought in customers for the house. She kept everyone in line: my grandmother, the hos, and the johns. I was told that Aunt Hattie had almost died from a drug overdose, but unlike my mom, she was resuscitated. After Aunt Hattie almost overdosed, she changed from being a tough street woman to a God-fearing Christian woman.

I am not certain what happened to my mother, but I did not attend a funeral. Aunt Hattie took us from the house that day and decided to raise us as her own. She introduced me to church and I was eventually baptized. She made me and Porchia attend Sunday school and church every Sunday. I even went to Bible study on Wednesdays. She also taught me some basic things about being a woman and taking care of myself, everything from hygiene to making sure no one took advantage of me. She would have some funny sayings like, "Mystery, when the chips are down, put all your money on God."

I had no friends because I was usually confined to the house. Although I was enrolled in school before I got pregnant, I rarely went because I did not understand any of my classes, and no one seemed to care if I was there or not. When I showed up at school, the girls always wanted to fight me for no reason that I knew about. I stayed to myself most of the time. Aunt Hattie told me that every woman needs at least one good friend. I met a girl from church, Nikki, who became my good friend. She also had a baby and lived with relatives.

Our stories were very similar with the exception that she lived with her aunt and uncle. Her uncle was a drunk and liked to beat up on women when he got drunk. Nikki had taken a couple of really good beatings and she wanted to find a place of her own for her and her baby.

Nikki asked me one day to come with her to an audition. She said she was going to be a dancer. I heard about places where people danced for money, but I had not ever seen one so I decided to go with Nikki. I was not prepared for what I saw when we entered the club. There were naked women everywhere. They were serving men drinks, they were sitting in men's laps, they were dancing on poles, and they were kissing each other. I just stood and looked at everything going on around me.

Some man came up to us and asked us what we wanted. Nikki told him that we were there to see Big John. The man asked us how old we were. Nikki was 17, but had previously warned me that we had to say we were 18 because neither one of us would be able to get into the club otherwise. Although I was only thirteen, I could pass for eighteen because I was tall and had developed a lot of tits and ass after Porchia was born.

The man said okay and asked us to follow him. He led us through several doors to the back of the club. We finally entered a door where a muscular-looking guy who favored Dwayne "The Rock" Johnson was sitting behind the desk.

Nikki said, "Hi, Big John, we talked on the phone. My cousin Dre sent me here."

Big John, whose name was fitting, came from behind his desk to give us both a thorough look-over. He asked us to follow him. He led us into another back room and began playing music. He looked directly at me and said with his deep voice, "Show me what you got."

I quickly blurted, "Oh no, I am not here for a job."

"Why not? You look like you got what it takes. Just do a little dance for me."

I hesitated, and then thought what the heck, why not? I started dancing like the people I saw on TV, and Big John asked me to slow it down.

He looked up and said, "Wait, I got an idea. Stay here." He left the room and came back with a girl. "Now do what she does." I copied what she was doing and this must have pleased Big John because he had a big smile on his face. He looked at me and said, "You are hired. Come back tomorrow at 7:00 p.m."

Nikki looked at him and said, "What about me?"

"I only need one," Big John said as he left the room.

I was so excited that I was going to be working that I ran home and told Aunt Hattie that I had a job. She was not happy about me dancing, but she understood that I was doing what I thought I needed to do to properly care for Porchia.

Aunt Hattie said, "Baby, just don't sell your soul to the devil."

I don't know what that meant when she said it, but I lost my friend Nikki and as it turned out, none of the girls at The Club would talk to me. They claimed I stole their loyal clients. I was just being me, and I did not care what they said because I was bringing in the money. I remember the first week I probably brought home four hundred dollars. By the next week I brought eight hundred dollars home. I thought I was doing pretty well for someone who did not even make it to junior high school. As time went by, I would not only dance, but perform sex acts for high profile clients in the Private Room. It was easy to make money because everything I did was for my baby. I did not mind as long as she had a chance to be somebody and not become part of the Dubois Curse.

Aunt Hattie watched Porchia at night. During the day, I played with and held my baby all day. I remember when I would hold Porchia for long periods of times and Aunt Hattie would say, "Mystery, put that chile down. You spoiling her. And I am not going to do that when you're not here."

Truth be told, Aunt Hattie spoiled her rotten. By the time Porchia turned 14 months, she was more than a handful. She was sassy and did not listen to anything I told her to do. She bonded with Aunt Hattie more than she did with me. Almost every night Porchia, although she had her own room with her own bed, slept with Aunt Hattie.

I sometimes felt like I was an outsider looking at my daughter being raised by another person. But I was so proud because she was talking and using full sentences by the time she was eighteen months. She would carry on a conversation like a grown woman. I knew my baby would be somebody one day.

One morning I came home from The Club and Aunt Hattie blurted out, "Honey, I quit my job because I know it is hard for you to work all night then come home to take care of a toddler. And you know Baby Girl is a handful."

Aunt Hattie cleaned houses for rich folks, but she quit working when Porchia was two-and-a-half years old. I believe she wanted to make certain that she had more of a hand in raising Porchia because she thought I was not able to do it. During this time, we decided to make up the story that Porchia was my cousin and her mom had died of cancer shortly after she was born.

She was right about one thing: Baby Girl was a handful, and it was not getting easier. I remember when Porchia was three years old and she came out doing a stripper routine and I almost lost my mind. That was the first time since her birth that I thought I would actually beat her. Aunt Hattie had to calm me down.

"Mystery, Baby Girl is just imitating what she sees on TV. I told you that we need to watch her every move. She changes the channels from cartoons to *Soul Train*."

"Aunt Hattie, I can't watch her 24-7. You know that child has a mind of her own."

"Yes, much like your grandmother."

"No, Aunt Hattie, nothing like my grandmother. Porchia is smart."

"So was your grandmother. She was a successful businesswoman."

"Well, Porchia will be a legal and smart businesswoman."

"I am sure she will, but you have to stop putting so much pressure on her. She is only a baby."

I realized I was probably being a little hard on her, but I did not want her to inherit any of my family's characteristics. I changed Porchia's legal last name from "DuBois" to "Williams" so she would take on

Aunt Hattie's name. I would do everything in my power to make sure the DuBois Curse ended with me.

Aunt Hattie made certain Porchia was surrounded by the right folks. She arranged for one of the young girls from church to tutor Porchia Monday through Thursday in return for one of Aunt Hattie's "slap-yo'-mama" meals. She also bought her reading, math, and science videos and games. Thanks to all of Aunt Hattie's efforts, when Porchia entered kindergarten, she could read and write.

By the time Porchia entered grade school, I felt completely alienated from my daughter. Aunt Hattie was doing an excellent job in raising her, so I was happy just to be around as her cousin. Our secret was kept between me, Aunt Hattie, and Duke, Porchia's father, who later became Pastor Charles. I thought I would never be able to forgive him for what he did to me, but I had a beautiful child who was going to break the DuBois Curse.

Chapter 2

I was the money maker at the club and I had a lot of responsibility for the success of The Club. I not only took care of myself, but I had to train the other girls. I gained respect from the girls and although they might not have liked me, they knew I wanted everyone to be successful.

Big John passed on management of The Club to one of his brothers, Jake, who received the job after being released from prison. Jake was a very handsome guy who all the girls at The Club wanted. Unlike Big John, he was very charming and flirtatious. He made all the girls feel like they were princesses.

Jake had gone to prison for killing a notorious drug dealer, which he claimed to be self-defense. Because of this murder, he was respected on the streets and known as one not to mess with. Jake, although on probation, carried his nine at all times so patrons would never get out of hand. The Club was a comfortable place to work and by this time, I was easily bringing home $2000 a week. I was doing quite well for a seventeen-year-old drop out.

One night while I was working in The Club, Jake told me I had a request in the Private Room. The Private Room is where we entertained high profile people like celebrities, athletes, politicians, etc., usually by appointment only. There was a special entrance so they would not be seen by any of our other patrons. I became the number one dancer for the Private Room. At any given weekend, I could easily make $1500 from the Private Room alone. I would never turn down a request for the Private Room because I had been saving up for Porchia's college fund. It was clear to me that she was a little genius who would definitely be attending some fancy college. However, I rarely received requests for the Private Room on a Tuesday night.

I walked into the room and saw Pastor Charles, formerly known as Duke the Man, sitting with a big smile on his face. I had not seen Duke face-to-face since he had raped me years ago. True, I attended church, but I took any means necessary to avoid any personal contact with him. Thanks to Aunt Hattie, I had long ago forgiven him for what he had done to me.

Duke looked up at me and said, "Hey, Precious."

"What are you doing here, Duke?"

"I see you sitting in the congregation every Sunday and I just wanted to be up close and personal."

"Why now, Duke?"

"You have my first child and I thought that we could reunite somehow. And what a beautiful child she is."

"Do you remember what you did to me?"

"Yes, and I am sorry for that. But you are all grown now so I don't see why we can't have a reunion?"

"We can't! And I never want you to come here again. My daughter does not know that you are her father. And it needs to stay that way."

"I want it to stay that way too, Precious. I just want to spend time with you."

"It will be a cold day in hell before I sleep with you."

He got up and pulled me toward him and said, "This is that day, 'cause you will do what the hell I tell you to do!"

I started struggling to get away from him, screaming, "Stop!"

Little did he know that there was a camera in the room and before I could say "stop" again, two of The Club's bouncers crashed into the room with one of them holding a gun to his head.

I was really shaken for the remainder of the night. Jake told me I needed the rest of the night off and he would take me out for dinner and drinks. At dinner, Jake apologized for what happened because he was the one that had led Pastor Charles to me. I tried to tell him that it was not his fault, and there was no way he could have known what would happen.

His response was, "Yeah, but I knew him back in da day and should have known he was up to no good coming to The Club."

We had several drinks and by the end of the night, I was in Jake's bed. I woke up the next morning and

Jake was not in the room. I was embarrassed about sleeping with the boss. Next thing I knew, Jake entered the room with a breakfast tray with biscuits, eggs, bacon, cappuccino, and orange juice.

"Hey, Sleeping Beauty."

"Jake, what'cha doing?"

"Bringing you breakfast."

"Jake, I need to get home to my daughter," I accidentally blurted out.

"Mystery, you don't have no daughter. You don't have to make things up to leave," Jake said, laughing.

"You are right. This is sort of embarrassing for me."

"Why?" asked Jake.

"'Cause I slept with you and we work together."

"Mystery, you neva noticed a brutha diggin' you?"

"No. You flirt with all the girls."

"Yeah, but you are the one who gets the special attention."

I was not trying to hear him. I was more concerned that I was not home yet and Aunt Hattie would be worried.

"Jake, I need to get home."

"Oh, you gonna blow a brutha off?"

"No. Can we talk about this later?" I asked.

"Right," he mumbled.

I forgot I had ridden with him. "Jake, can you take me to get my car?"

"Yeah!" he snapped.

The drive to The Club was quiet. I did not want to hurt his feelings, but I did not want to mess up our working relationship either. I know in the past when stuff like this happened the guy would get a little possessive and the woman could not make her money. I am all about making money for me, Aunt Hattie, and Porchia. Besides maintaining household expenses, Porchia attended after school programs so that she could be ahead of everyone else at school. I was struggling to maintain because of the costs of all her activities which also included sports camps and little league basketball teams.

We pulled up and Jake said, "Forget about what happened."

"Jake, I like you, but you are my boss."

"It's cool. I'll see you tonight," said Jake.

"Yes you will, Boss," I said before departing.

Damn, why did I sleep with him? I hope he does not hold it against me. I did not know that he liked me that way. Hopefully everything will go back to normal. I was thinking about how I could make things better on my drive home. I must not have been paying attention because I rear-ended the Cadillac in front of me. An old lady got out of the car cussing at me, saying that she had only had the car for a week and I had destroyed it.

The car had a slight dent in the bumper, but my hooptie was tore up. I had bought a used Corolla to get me to The Club and around town, but it was on its last legs. I told the screaming woman that I would pay her for all of her damages. I asked her to follow me to the bank so I could give her cash for any damages caused. She told me that she did not know if I had enough to pay her in cash. I went to the bank and pulled out $3000 and she seemed happy.

I arrived home and Aunt Hattie was waiting for me. I walked in and said, "I am sorry, Aunt Hattie. I had some issues last night."

"Well, I guess so! You did not even think to call? I was worried sick about you. It is not like you to just not show up. I called the hospitals, the morgues, the jails. Girl, what is wrong with you?"

"It's a long story." The truth was she adored Pastor Charles and I did not want to upset her so I said, "Did Porchia get off to school alright?"

"Yes, she did. But she noticed that you were not here and asked about you."

"She did? She does not seem to care if I am dead or alive."

"Mystery, you know she is a growing girl and they are different animals."

"Yeah, but she seems to still love you."

"And she loves you too. She just has a different way of showing it."

"Well, Aunt Hattie, if you don't mind I need to take a shower."

"Go ahead, baby. For some reason, I think you need to cleanse yourself," Aunt Hattie said.

While showering, it hit me that I needed to get a new car. I was not prepared to buy a new car now. That was when I got the idea to take advantage of what had happened last night at The Club.

"Well hello, Pastor Charles."

"Who is this?"

"Yo' baby mama."

"Why are you calling me after you almost got me killed last night?"

"I have a proposition for you."

"Oh, I see you are just like your mama."

"I need $35,000 deposited to my account tomorrow."

"Bitch, you crazy? You must be on crack!" he screamed.

"I will get $35,000 deposited to my account by tomorrow or your wife will know everything, including what you did last night."

"I can't get $35,000 tomorrow!" he shouted.

"You know, the more I think about it, I don't need $35,000. I need $40,000 or the church will know what you did to me when I was only 11 years old. Oh, by the way, every time you say that you can't, it will go up by $5000. I will text you my account information. I will check my account at 3:00 p.m. Additionally, I need for you to get an insurance policy with Porchia's name on it. I will also text you her information. If all of these terms are not met, say goodbye to the world as you know it. By the way, it was a pleasure seeing you last night."

That was the first time in my life I felt in complete control of what happened around me and I realized that I did not have to be the victim. I loved my new, fully-loaded red Volvo sitting on 20's. I also received a UPS package with insurance policy information,

$750,000 payable to Porchia in the event of Duke's death. That was the least he could do for her.

Chapter 3

Porchia was my little princess that I loved and adored from afar. I attended all of her open houses, holiday plays, and parent-teacher conferences with Aunt Hattie. One of my proudest moments was watching her advance to win the State Spelling Bee Championship, then go on to win third place at the national competition. I remember her being very sad after that competition. We told her that we wanted to take her out to celebrate her win. She told us she did not want to go. When asked why, she looked at us and with big crocodile tears in her eyes and said, "The only winner is first place. Everyone else are merely losers."

By the time she entered fifth grade she told me that she did not want me to come to her school anymore because the children made fun of her. I will never forget that conversation. Standing with her hands on her hips, shaking her head from side to side, and rolling her eyes, she said, "Mystery, please stay away from my school."

"Porchia, why do you want me to stay away from your school?" I asked.

"Well, the kids say that you are a ho and that I will be a ho just like you."

I was so hurt because that is what I was attempting to keep from happening all of these years. The DuBois Curse was trying to take over my daughter in the fifth grade.

"Porchia, those kids are just being mean. I am a dancer."

"Yeah, but they said you take off your clothes to dance for money and that constitutes that you are a ho," she said as if she was stating an important fact.

I did not know what the hell "constitute" meant, but I knew that I was not prepared to go into a conversation about ho'in', so I agreed to stay away from her school.

At that time, I felt I was being pushed further and further away from my daughter's life. Anytime something exciting or bad happened, she would run straight to Aunt Hattie. When I would try to ask her about it, she would look at me and say, "Mystery, it is too difficult for you to comprehend." It was like she spoke a foreign language at ten years old. She would use words that I needed a dictionary to understand.

I noticed a complete change in her by the time she entered middle school. Her speech changed from those words that I would have to look up in a dictionary to talking like everyone else in the hood. She would lash out at me for any and all reasons. Our relationship eventually became like that of sisters who did not like each other. I would hurt each time she said something cruel, yelled, or cursed at me. There were many times I was close to saying, "Look, girl, you can't talk to me like that because I am your mother!" But that wouldn't be want I wanted. I knew I had to control the DuBois Curse.

We all went to Sunday school and church every Sunday, but by the time Porchia entered the seventh grade she did not want to attend anymore. She would say things like, "God is a farce." I was not certain what a farce was but I knew it was not good because of other things she would say.

I would look at Aunt Hattie and she would just shake her head and say to Porchia, "Baby Girl, one day you are going to learn that can't nobody do you like Jesus."

I know my mother and grandmother did not attend church, but they definitely believed in God. I am not certain where Porchia got all of her thoughts, but she was definitely not like anyone I knew when it came to believing in God. I often wondered what did she hear when she went to Sunday school and church as a child.

During this time Porchia also grew really tall and became fanatic about basketball. I questioned whether my daughter was going to be a lesbian because she acted more like a little boy than a little girl. I worked with several lesbians at The Club, but they were all very girly. I have had sex with women in The Private Room, but it was all about pleasing the man and getting paid. But my daughter seemed to have little interest in things girls her age would have interest and she enjoyed hanging out with boys. While we attended church, Porchia would sit around watching football then head out to the park to play basketball with the guys.

But it did not seem like she had any romantic interest in boys either. I tried to have a conversation with her about sex when she was thirteen. She looked at me, rolled her eyes, and said, "Mystery, there ain't nothing about sex I wanna hear from a ho."

That was the second time I remembered wanting to beat her down. But with all that attitude, I still loved her and wanted to protect her from the Curse.

Porchia wanted to become more and more involved with sports, but I used my money to make it clear that she would have to keep up her grades too. Our agreement was that she spend as much time studying as she did with basketball, volleyball, and softball. She soon realized that she was doing too much and dropped the other sports to focus on basketball and her grades.

After attending her basketball games in middle school, I then realized that she was very good at it and could support her decision to play that sport. However, if it was only up to me, she would concentrate on just her grades. Playing basketball would not get her anything out of life. The only way to escape the DuBois Curse was to go to college, earn a degree, and get a high-paying job, something like a doctor or lawyer.

Chapter 4

The more I wanted to be a part of Porchia's life, the more she pushed me away. She started hanging out with a girl named Chanti and, to my surprise, her sister Tracy. Tracy was Duke's daughter by his wife, Ms. Carletta. It was so hard watching them hang out and not tell them that they were sisters. When Tracy first came over to visit, I asked how they had met. It turned out that some girls wanted to beat up Tracy because she thought she was better than everyone else because her father was a big-time preacher. Porchia stepped in and told the girls they would have to come through her first. Porchia was known to be hot-headed and she could back up what she said, so the girls backed down. Ever since then, they had been the best of friends.

With Porchia living her own life, I decided it was time for me to live my life. I started dating for the very first time. I met many men at The Club that wanted to take me out. But unlike many of the girls that worked at The Club that said that "the world was their playground", I believed that I should never "shit in the pot that pays me." So I was not down for dating any of the patrons. I knew everybody in the Ward and none

23

of those guys interested me. Most of the guys at church were either married or gay. I did not get out to socialize outside of The Club. So I thought that my only means to meet eligible men was to go through an online dating site. Also I knew a couple of girls who had met their guys online.

I tried all of the sites that people told me about, like *BlackPeopleMeet, PlentyofFish,* also *BlackSingles, Match.com,* and *ChristianSingles,* but nothing seemed to work for me. I met men looking for booty calls, African scammers, women, unemployed men, men in other countries, men just released from prison, and the list goes on. That is, until I found *Sugardaddie.com.*

I actually thought that this website was a joke but it really had men looking for women to spoil. The first guy I met was in the import/export business. Although I had never dated a white man, I was willing to give it a try. I could not believe it when he said he was going to pick me up so that we could spend a weekend in San Diego. I had to quickly let him know that weekends were not good for me, but I was available Sunday through Tuesday. I never worked on Sundays, and Monday and Tuesday were slow days. I figured Jake would not mind me taking off a couple of days.

We arranged to meet on Sunday. It was obvious that this man had posted a pic of his son or someone else because when he showed up he was much balder, older, and shorter. But I was quickly able to ignore his looks when we pulled up to his private jet. His jet looked like a small commuter plane but with comfortable big leather loveseats, tables, a stocked bar, big screen televisions, and a stereo system. I never realized that planes were made like this. We ate fancy appetizers that I can't remember how to say or spell and drank some expensive champagne. By the time we landed in San Diego, he started favoring George Clooney.

I spent two days living the life of a celebrity. We went to parties, ate at fine restaurants, and drove up to Los Angeles to attend a Lakers game, where we had front row seats. You could see that he was proud to have me on his arm. He introduced me to all his friends as his girlfriend. I smiled and played the part. I avoided having conversation with his people because I knew that we did not have much in common. I pretty much answered questions that they asked and kept it at that. When they asked me what I did, I told them that I managed a nightclub in Houston. That seemed to go over well and was not far from the truth.

I did not realize that people partied so hard on Mondays and Tuesdays. I had to wonder what most of these people did for a living. Everywhere we went they were freely pouring expensive liquor, and people were snorting cocaine like it grew on trees. I was exhausted by the time we arrived back in Houston after partying all night and fighting him off from having sex during the day. He attempted to make our next date and I had to tell him that this arrangement would not work for me.

My first date was not that bad so I thought I would try it again. I met this Latino guy from NYC who was on a business trip in Houston for a month. I saw several pictures and he appeared to be very handsome. We communicated through texts for a while before being able to meet up. We finally made arrangements to have dinner. After my first experience, I knew it was best to meet him versus allowing him to pick me up at my house. I agreed to meet him at one of the downtown restaurants.

I looked around the restaurant for him because the only guy I saw was a man wearing a button-down light green shirt that exposed his hairy chest and big medallions hanging from his neck. His hair was filled with something that made it puff forward like Elvis's hair. He had on yellow skinny jeans and sandals.

He saw me looking and said, "Hi, are you Myster-ee?"

My first thought was to say "NO", but I looked around to see if there was possibly anyone who knew me in the restaurant. It looked like it would be a safe place, so I said, "Are you Jorge?"

He smiled, took my hand, kissed it, and said, "You are even more beautiful than your pics."

I thought to myself, *I wish I could say the same.* But we had good conversation, great food, and expensive wine. Against my better judgment, I agreed to go with him to a nightclub located near the restaurant.

I never go to downtown clubs, but it was cool. They were playing decent music - not the type I would normally listen to, but I was digging it and he was buying drinks. Taylor Swift's song "Shake it Off" came on and this man grabbed me, saying, 'C'mon, this is my song!'

There was an empty dance floor and he got out there and started doing a John Travolta *Saturday Night Fever* routine. I stood there in complete shock. My feet were glued to the floor and I could not move. He was so into his dance, he did not notice I was not dancing. I stayed frozen until he finished his performance.

When we got back to the table, the waitress came up to the table and said, "Hey, Mystery, are you going to introduce me to your man?"

I looked up and it was Kitty, one of the girls from The Club. I wish I could have just vanished into thin air. I gave her my "get-the-fuck-out-of-my-face" look.

But that seemed to hype her up even more because she looked at me and said, "So what are you drinking? I think we have a special on the John Travolta drink."

I responded, "No, bring me your 'Fuck Off' drink." I stood up, looked at Jorge, and said, "It was nice meeting you," and walked out of the club. I don't believe in three strikes and you are out, so I swore off online dating forever.

Chapter 5

Porchia grew up right before my eyes, and without me having a place in her life anymore. By the time she entered high school, I was Enemy #1. The more I tried to be there for her, the more she let me know she did not like me nor respect me, and that she did not want to have anything to do with me. I told Aunt Hattie that she needed to talk with her about the way she treated me.

Aunt Hattie said, "Well, baby, she does not like that you are a stripper."

"Aunt Hattie, does she know that stripping is what allows her to go to her basketball camps, her trips that she takes, buys her all of those electronic gadgets she likes, pays for extracurricular activities, buys the clothes on her back, pays her medical bills, and puts food in her mouth? I don't buy me things because I'm saving up for her college fund."

"Baby, I know it is a strained relationship. But you have chosen to protect her from your past. That was your decision. You will have to become stronger in your faith and believe that everything will be okay. Pray on it. Ask God to give you the guidance you need to have a healthy, loving relationship with Porchia. But you have to realize, the choice you made will never allow you to have a mother-daughter relationship with her."

"Aunt Hattie, at this point, I will be happy if she did not curse at me or call me out of my name."

"I will talk to her about that. Baby Girl should not disrespect you that way. But you need to take responsibility for your part in the relationship. I love you both and just want for our family to be a strong, loving family. With God on our side, we can do that."

Porchia walked in from school as Aunt Hattie and I were having our conversation. "What are you two all huddled up about. Mystery have you fucked up again?"

"Baby Girl, have you lost your mind? You know I don't tolerate that type of language around me!"

"Sorry, Aunt Hattie. I guess I thought I was still on the basketball court," said Porchia, making faces behind Aunt Hattie's back.

"Well, keep that language on the court, child. You ain't too big for me to spank. And you need to apologize to Mystery."

"For what?"

I interrupted their bantering. "Hey, Porchia, I have tickets to go see the Rockets. Do you want to go?"

"With you?" Porchia asked with a frown on her face.

"Yes, with me."

"Nah I'ma pass!"

"Well, if you don't want to go with me I have two tickets and you can take one of your friends."

"Where are the seats?" Porchia asked.

"Floor seats, of course," I said.

"When?"

"Sunday," I responded.

"You need to be providing her seats to church on Sunday," interrupted Aunt Hattie.

"No, Aunt Hattie, you would not want that! I would go in singing, "You a fake, Pastor. You can't conceal it. You know how I know? 'Cause I can feel it. You're a fake, Pastor. No rhyme or reason. 'Cause in your mind, it's lyin' season'," Porchia said, singing and dancing around the kitchen.

She was dead on talking about her dad. He was a phony. I thought he was okay, but after that encounter I had with him years back, I never trusted him again. I definitely kept my distance. I started to join another church, but did not know what I would say to Aunt Hattie about me leaving Better Hope Tabernacle. She had so much love for the man and I did not want to disappoint her. His entire congregation acted as if he walked on water. His wife and family just adored him. If they only knew.

"Baby Girl, you need to stop it," said Aunt Hattie.

"No, Aunt Hattie, he needs to stop it. Why is this preacher rolling new Caddies every year, living in a big house, wearing thousand dollar suits, sporting fancy jewelry, and taking trips out of the country flying first class every three months when he ain't got a job; while the people around him are struggling every day? Some of them can't afford electricity, new clothes, or food, but yet, they are willing to give their last dollar to him. That's what I call a PIMP!" shouted Porchia.

I had to laugh. That girl was the feistiest child I had ever seen! "So Porchia, do you want the tickets? If not, I will find someone who does."

"Okay, let me go call Chanti to see if she wants to go," responded Porchia.

"Let me know soon."

Porchia left the kitchen singing, "You a fake..."

Aunt Hattie looked at me and whispered, "That's yo' child."

It turned out that neither Chanti nor Tracy could make the game, but Porchia really wanted to go see the Spurs play the Rockets. One of her favorite players was Tim Duncan so she decided she would let me take her. This was the first time in a long time that Porchia and I had the chance to do anything alone. I was just happy to be with my little girl. She became really excited after she saw that we were sitting right behind the San Antonio bench. She was even happier when I arranged for her to meet some of her favorite players. I wish I could make every day like this for her. She thanked me over and over and told me it was the most fun she had in a long time. It felt good to do something right in her eyes. I was just glad that I had clients that could make that happen.

My joy was short-lived when the next day Porchia came home from school early.

"Porchia, why are you home so early?" I asked.

"Because I was fighting your battles!"

"Girl, what are you talking about?'

"This chick at school said you broke up her mom and dad 'cause you were screwing her dad. She said you were the lowest of low hos and I looked just like you, and probably will be just like you."

"Porchia, I am so tired of you getting into silly fights."

"Well if you weren't ho'in', I probably would not have to get into fights."

"Porchia, I dance for a living. You know that. I can't help it if women are jealous of me. I am not messing with anyone's husband. They come to see me, I don't go to see them. If she lost her dad, believe me, it was not because of me. That was between her mom and her dad."

"Mystery why can't you go find a normal job? A grocery store checker…a waitress…a barista."

"A b-what?" I asked.

"Never mind. Any job that does not involve you taking off your clothes."

"It is not that easy, Porchia. I spend all my money making sure that you have the chance that I never had."

"That is not your responsibility. I will be fine without the money you spend."

"Girl, how do you think you have a place that you can lay your nappy head down?" I shouted.

"Tramp, just do you! Where is Aunt Hattie?"

"Don't talk to me like that. I will lay you out."

"Try it," Porchia said while walking away.

I was at a loss when it came to Porchia. I had to talk to someone besides Aunt Hattie, who thought prayer took care of everything. I believe in God, but many times He don't answer my prayers fast enough for me.

I went to my laptop to look for counselors. I was going to take Aunt Hattie's advice. I had to take responsibility for things that happened in our relationship. I realized I could not put all the blame on Porchia.

Chapter 6

I found a counselor who specialized in child-parent relationships. I made an appointment to see Dr. Frazier. I had never done anything like this. I knew people that went to shrinks because they were crazy. I knew that I was not crazy; I just needed help with Porchia. I was so close to telling her that I was her mother, but I also knew that it was only the Dubois Curse messing with me. It was bad enough that people gave her a bad time about me being her cousin. How would they treat her if they found out that in fact, I was her mother? I could never let that happen. I could not allow the DuBois Curse to win.

I wondered what Dr. Frazier would think about me. I wonder if she would understand what I was attempting to do for Porchia. I hoped that she was a parent and she could understand how I felt as a mother. I did not know how much I could share or not share with her. I thought about all of this for hours before my afternoon appointment with her. I picked up the phone four times to cancel the appointment, but realized I needed to do everything in my power to improve my relationship with Porchia.

When I arrived at the office, it was a very nice plush office with a big aquarium with all types of fancy fish on an entire part of one wall. There were fancy seating and elevator music playing in the waiting room. I walked in and the receptionist said, "Good afternoon, Miss. May I help you?"

I was surprised to see a black female receptionist. In this fancy office, I thought everybody would be white. She actually spoke like a white person and not the black people in the Ward.

I thought I would attempt to speak properly also. "Well herlo, ma'am. I have a one o'clock apertment with Dr. Frasher." I think that is how Madea would do it. She gave me an odd look then asked me my name. I answered, "I am Miss Dooboooy."

"Yes, I see that you have a 1:15 appointment with Dr. Frazier, Miss Dubois. Do you mind filling out these papers and returning them to me? I will let Dr. Frazier know that you are here."

I took the papers but did not understand a lot of stuff they were asking. I had not really learned to read or write. I stared at the papers for a while.

"Can I assist you with something, Miss DuBois?" asked the receptionist.

"Yes. I have this disease where I read backwards and it is hard for me to fill out papers."

"Oh, I apologize. Do you have dyslexia?"

What is this snooty bitch talking about? I answered, "Yes. I think so."

36

"Okay, Miss, I can help you. I will ask you the questions, you can respond verbally, and I will write down the answers. Would that work for you?"

I just wanted to run out of the office. I responded, "Yes, that will work."

She went on to ask me a lot of questions that I thought were way too personal for anyone to be asking, but I answered because I knew I had to help mine and Porchia's relationship. After I was done being grilled, she told me I could have a seat and the doctor would be with me soon.

I thought to myself, *I hope the doctor is white and not stuck-up like this woman. Usually white people don't act that way toward a black person. But black people, especially black women with a little education, will act like their shit don't stank with another sista.* The doctor came out and I was about to pick up my bag and run. It was Kwame Frazier who grew up in the Ward. His folks owned the liquor store down the street from the house. He was about seven years older than me, but I knew all of his folks.

"Mystery?"

"Kwame?"

"Hey girl, you look good. It's nice to see you."

Before I realized it, I said, "I wish I could say the same."

"Come on. Let's go into my office."

I was not going to speak with Kwame about my problems with Porchia. He couldn't ever know that she was my daughter. I thought again about running, but I followed him back to his office. His office looked like a very fancy living room. It had a sofa, a love seat and some big chairs. He had it decorated in an antique fashion. He also had a big oversized desk that looked out onto a pond.

"I see you doing really good for yourself, Kwame."

"I enjoy helping people."

"And I see you must be getting paid for doing it."

"Mystery, so why are you here?"

"Kwame, this is not going to work. I know you and your family."

"I am a professional and there is something called doctor-patient confidentiality, which means I can't tell anyone what we discuss."

"Ain't there something called conflict of interest, where my interest conflicts with yours?"

"Mystery, if you feel uncomfortable speaking with me, I can refer you to one of my colleagues."

"Your what?"

"I can refer you to another person that does the same thing that I do."

"Yeah, that would be cool. I need to speak to someone that I don't know and someone who does not know me."

"That will work better for me too."

"Why does it work better for you?"

"Because now that you are not my patient, I can ask you out."

"Oh, so now you gonna try to get at me? You don't even know what I came here for. I might be 5150 and came here to talk about how I kill people I go out with," I said, smiling.

"Mystery, you may be a serial dater, but I know that you ain't no serial killer," he laughed.

I took my time to check out Kwame. He was attractive in an odd type of way. He still wore a high-top fade, his mustache was a little too thick, and his eyebrows looked like a bush, but I saw possibilities. Nothing that Joe down at the barbershop or Hopsung down at the nail shop could not handle.

"Ha! Doctor, you are funny. So do you have a business card?"

"Yes, but I would like to get your number so I can make sure that we keep in contact," he said while handing me his card.

"Do you usually get everything that you like?"

Kwame smiled and licked his lips. "Yes. Usually."

That move turned me on. I leaned closer toward him and said, "Me too." And with that, I got up and did my special sashay out of his door.

When I got to the car, I realized that I still didn't have what I needed to have a better relationship with Porchia; but I thought maybe that was my sign that I did not need to talk to anyone about it. I wondered whether this was a message from God. I sat in the car for about thirty minutes, wondering about what would be the best thing to do.

All of a sudden it clicked. Maybe if I went back to school, she would respect me. She treated me like I was the world's biggest dummy. I knew I couldn't read and write, but that was one of the reasons I pushed for her to do better. But just maybe, I thought, I could gain respect from her if I had my high school diploma.

It was difficult finding an adult school that I could attend during the day. Most of the programs were at night. I found a program at a community college that I could attend during the day that would allow me to get my high school diploma in three years. I was so excited that I went and registered that day. I had to wait a month before starting, but I was happy about the opportunity. I did not say anything to Porchia or Aunt Hattie because I wanted to surprise them once I earned my diploma.

I was leaving the campus, excited about my new opportunities, when my phone rang from a number I did not recognize. I did not have many friends, so I wondered who it could be. I had called a couple of programs that offered online courses, so maybe it was one of them returning my call.

"Hello, this is Mystery."

"Well hello there, Ms. Dubois."

"Who is this?"

"Oh, you forgot about me the minute you left my office?"

"Kwame? How did you get my number?"

"It was on the form that you completed."

"Isn't there some rule against that?" I asked.

"I don't think there is a rule against me wanting to take you out to dinner."

"I don't know. I am pretty busy."

"I am not asking for all your time. Just a couple of hours," Kwame responded.

"Okay. I will get back to you," I replied.

"If you don't, I know where to find you."

"Are you a stalker or something?" I asked.

"No, just trying to let you know that I am really interested in you," Kwame replied.

"You don't know me."

"No, but I am trying to get to know you."

"Okay, Kwame. Let's touch base on Tuesday."

"Dinner?"

"Sure," I said.

"My last appointment is at four o'clock. Would seven o'clock work?

"Sounds good."

"Okay. I will pick you up at seven. See you then," Kwame said.

Before I could say anything, he had hung up. I was going to tell him that I would meet him, but I forgot he already knew where I lived. He probably knew my history too, which made me wonder what made him interested in me, him being a big old doctor and everything, and it didn't look like he was doing bad at all. I would go to dinner, but that would be it. I knew I had to concentrate on getting my diploma. Working and going to school was more than I had ever done at one time.

When I got home I was happier than I had been in a long time. There was nothing that Porchia could say or do that would take me out of my happy space. When

I walked into the house, Aunt Hattie was sitting and watching TV in the living room.

"Hi, Aunt Hattie." I went over and kissed her.

"Hey, Mystery. Girl, what has got into you, or should I say, who?"

"Ooh, Aunt Hattie! I can't believe you said that."

"Girl, neither of us are virgins. What is going on?"

I did not want to tell Aunt Hattie about school. "Things are just looking up at The Club. I may be able to take on more of a management role."

This was true because Jake wanted to take on some type of music-producing project and he had spoken to me about managing The Club. I did not think that this would be possible now since I would be attending school.

"So what would you be doing?" asked Aunt Hattie.

"Not much more than I am doing right now. Probably more tasks like making sure the dancers are there, doing bookings, and stuff like that."

"Well, if anybody can do it, you can."

"Thanks, Aunt Hattie. I love you."

"I love you too, Mystery."

"Well, I have to go get ready for work. Where is Porchia?"

"She had basketball practice, tutoring after school, and then said she was hanging out with some of her basketball teammates. By the way, are you going to the game Friday night?"

"Yes, Aunt Hattie. I told you I would take you. I may need to leave the game early 'cause I have to go to work. You know Friday is a moneymaker."

"Well, I think Porchia really likes when you are there."

"Aunt Hattie, I said I would be there. I just can't stay through the entire game. What don't you understand about the responsibilities I have around here?"

"Baby, I know you make money down there at that club, but you could take one night off."

"Aunt Hattie, I can't talk about this right now. I have to take a shower."

"Okay, but just think about what you said about yours and Porchia's relationship."

"That is all I think about, Aunt Hattie," I said as I walked away from her to start getting ready for work.

Chapter 7

The day came for me to attend my first class and I was excited about going to school. I thought I was going to be the oldest in my class, but I was actually one of the youngest. There were a lot of older Latinos. This one lady there had to be older than Aunt Hattie. They encouraged me because I thought if they could do it, I certainly could do it. Everything seemed to be going great. I understood most of the subjects and for the things that I did not quite understand, Kwame provided me with extra help. We had been dating for a couple of months and he was supportive of everything that I did. He told me over and over that I could do anything that I put my mind to doing. The great thing about that was I believed him.

One thing that I really enjoyed about school was now I could understand Porchia a lot better. If she used words that I did not understand the meaning of, I could actually look them up in the dictionary because I understood the spelling. Our relationship was still strained, but I was feeling better about myself. When she started arguments, I no longer became defensive. I understood that she was going through growing pains, as Kwame helped me realize.

Kwame and I often talked about me trying to be a positive role model for my younger cousin. We worked together on different things that I could do to be supportive of Porchia. One technique that we practiced was called "mirroring." When there was a disagreement, instead of arguing about something, you repeated what you thought the person said in your own words before responding to something. If the person disagreed with the way you framed the statement, they could correct you. It worked well when it was just me and Kwame. When I tried it with Porchia, she said, "You sound like a parrot on crack." I decided to let that technique go.

At the same time, I was running The Club alone. Jake spent most of his time in the studio. He started a record label called H-Town Underground Records. He worked with a lot of underground rappers to bring their style of rap to mainstream. I came up with the idea to have some of his artists perform live while the girls did their routines on Fridays and Saturdays. The word got out on the street and The Club had a line around the block to get in. It was the hottest joint on this side of the Mississippi River.

When I was not at The Club or school, I spent most of my time with Kwame. I finally introduced Kwame to Porchia and Aunt Hattie. I was bragging to them that he was a doctor. Porchia started asking him all types of questions. That was the first time I realized that Kwame was not a doctor that went to medical school, but a doctor because he received a doctorate degree in counseling. Of course Porchia would not let me forget that I was telling everybody that he was a medical doctor.

After Kwame left, Porchia said, laughing, "Mystery, next time you turn a trick for a doctor, make sure that he is a real doctor." She seemed to take joy in any pain that she could inflict on me.

I realized that I did not know much about Kwame. Most of our time together was spent talking about me.

One day Kwame took me to one of Houston's most popular and expensive restaurants. During appetizers, I started asking questions and found out that Kwame was separated from his wife and his ten-year-old twin girls. I found out that they had been separated for six months. He dropped himself and said that they were going to counseling.

"So you and your wife are working on getting back together?" I asked.

"No, we are working on learning how to co-parent from separate households," he answered.

"So why did you and your wife split up?"

"She thought I was cheating."

"Were you?" I asked.

He hesitated before answering. "Yes, I was. But it is over now."

"Who were you cheating with?"

"Mystery that is old news. I have moved on from that."

"So why are you not answering?"

"Janay."

"Janay! Your receptionist?"

"Yes, and I said it was over."

"You know what, Kwame? There are some things I just did not know about you. I think we are moving too fast. We obviously need to get to know each other better."

"Mystery, I think you are overreacting."

"No, this is overreacting." I threw his house keys at him and then got up and left.

I was so done with men. I thought about carrying on a relationship with a woman but the relationships I saw between females were just as bad as the ones I saw between males and females, if not worse. Kwame was the first person I had ever been interested in as far as a relationship. No one else was even worth my time. I had no personal life, so I put my time mostly into The Club.

Big John had officially made me co-manager of The Club with Jake. Jake's record label had taken off and he spent maybe four days out of the month at The Club. His primary role was to take care of the financials for the club. I started Humpday Wednesdays where all drinks were half off. This night became another busy night for the club. By that time, I no longer danced unless it was a Private Room request.

After starting Humpday Wednesdays, some of my long-time patrons requested that I open up on Wednesday. I thought it was a good idea for me to open, but instead of opening up on Wednesdays, I decided to have Throwback Thursdays where I would do a routine for our patrons. My ideas had the club earning more money than they ever had. Jake started referring to me as the business mogul because of some of the ideas I incorporated at The Club.

Yes, I learned words like "mogul" attending school. English and math were my favorite subjects. I started thinking about going to business school. I realized I enjoyed doing what I was doing at The Club and I thought that maybe I could open up my own business one day. It was more than just making the money; it was creating the ideas to make the money that excited me.

I had already put a year into my classes, but I decided to take the GED so I could start business classes at the community college. I found the perfect program called the Business Management Entrepreneurship certificate. It would only take me one year to complete and I would learn things like marketing, business law, and accounting.

Porchia was busy with school and basketball. She was one of the leading players on her team. She played on the varsity team as a sophomore. My little girl was growing up to be a fine young lady. She still did not pay me much attention and she enjoyed picking fights. I did not know what I could do to earn her respect, but

I felt really good about myself and the direction of my life.

Aunt Hattie did not seem to be her regular spunky self these days. I worried about her and had conversations with her about taking care of herself. Aunt Hattie was still cooking greens with fatback. We would go shopping and I attempted to substitute some of her meats for healthy stuff like turkey.

She told me on one shopping trip, "Girl, we all gotta die from something. I am going die eating the food I want." There was no point in arguing with Aunt Hattie because besides Porchia, cooking was her passion.

Aunt Hattie told me I had been working too much. She started the conversation by saying, "Mystery, you have been spending your days and nights at the club. Is there really something else going on? Are you seeing someone?"

I am not certain why she always thought a man had to be involved. The truth was that I had not been in a relationship since I had walked away from Kwame at that restaurant a few months back. I did not even have time to think about men or relationships because I was concentrating on making myself worthy and respectable for my daughter. Aunt Hattie thought I was spending days and night at the club, but I was not ready to discuss what I was doing during the day. I did not want to disappoint anyone just in case I did not succeed. Porchia already thought very little of me, and I just wanted to make them both very proud.

Because I knew Aunt Hattie felt that I was not spending enough time at home, I planned a vacation for the three of us to New Orleans during Porchia's spring break. I booked us rooms at the Ritz Carlton in the French Quarters. I was so excited. I set up massages for us, arranged for a tour of the bayou, and made reservations at Emeril's. Aunt Hattie watched a lot of cooking shows and she was always talking about Chef Emeril Lagasse. I thought it would be great to surprise her by going to his restaurant.

When I spoke to Porchia about it, she rolled her eyes and said, "You are supposed to be paying for me to go to basketball camp."

I had totally forgotten. "Porchia, you can take a break from basketball for a week."

"No, I can't. I can't be like you. I need to go to college, and the only way I will get there is through scholarships. And I need to perfect my game to get my scholarship."

She did not know I had been saving up for her schooling since she was two years old. I had over $400,000 in the bank for her college fund. I wanted her to go to a top school, so most of my money went towards savings to ensure that she would get a good education. I failed to share this information with Porchia because I still wanted her to work hard, at least on her academic subjects.

"Porchia, how much is it?"

"I gave you the information over a month ago. If you did not spend so much time ho'in', you probably would know all of this."

I started to pull my weight and tell her I didn't have the money, but this probably would have just upset her more. I did not want to go on vacation with her cussing at me the entire time. "I don't know what I did with it. I am sorry. Can you let me know the cost so I can get money to pay for it?" I responded.

"Thanks, Mystery."

I was so shocked to hear those two words come out of her mouth. She rarely thanked me for anything these days. I spoke to Aunt Hattie and she came up with the idea for us to go and let Porchia stay with Tracy. I told her, "I can't allow her to spend a night under that man's roof."

"Mystery, I thought you had forgiven him."

"Yes, Aunt Hattie. He has long ago been forgiven. But what he did to me will never be forgotten."

Although I was not comfortable with the idea, Porchia asked to stay with Chanti. Porchia never stayed overnight at anyone's house. I was even more uncomfortable because Chanti's mom, Cherelle, was Big John's girlfriend. I did not like my little girl staying where there was a possibility she would be around drugs. I knew that our entire hood was full of drugs and I worked around drugs, but I did not invite that into our personal lives. My mother was a drug addict that I saw die at an early age.

I spoke with Cherelle and she ensured me that no illegal activity took place at her house. She also told me that she would be around to supervise the girls. I must admit that I liked and respected Big John, despite his career choice. He seemed to be a responsible person. I mentioned to him that my cousin would be staying with Cherelle for a couple days and he said, "Don't worry. She will be in good hands."

Aunt Hattie and I drove to New Orleans and she had a good time. She reminded me of the old Aunt Hattie that was around when I was a child. We went to the restaurants and clubs on Bourbon Street. We took our bayou trip, where we saw alligators up close and personal. Our spa experience was better than any sex that I had had lately.

We spent six hours at the spa where we received a massage, a facial, a scrub, a wrap, and lunch. All of the stress that had been building up in me for years seemed to be released in one session. I had never received a massage, but I knew that this was something that I had to add to my pampering list. But the favorite part of Aunt Hattie's trip was meeting Emeril. She talked about it all the way back to Houston. I had never seen Aunt Hattie use her cell phone, but she called her friends to let them know as well. Although we had a great time, I was anxious to get back to Porchia.

Chapter 8

Getting back to the realities of life did not go as well as I expected. It started with Porchia carrying three Macy's bags, very excited that Chanti's boyfriend, Sweezy, had taken them both shopping. I was not fond of the thought that a drug dealer was taking my teenage daughter shopping.

"Porchia, you don't need to accept clothing from anyone. If you want something, I can buy it for you."

"Don't worry, Mystery. I am not like you. I don't ho fa clothes. But if I did, it's none of your business."

"Look, I am not trying to start a fight. I am just letting you know that if you need something, you can come to me."

"Thank you for your concern and generosity. Oh, in case you are stuck, generosity means kindness," said Porchia mockingly.

Aunt Hattie looked at both of us and said, "I just enjoyed the best time I have had in a long time. Please don't either of you ruin it. Can you all just talk to each other like human beings?"

I wanted to say that I had been nothing but civil to her. The girl seemed to hate me for no good reason at all. So what if I was a stripper? I still deserved to be treated with respect, especially since I was the one who made certain all of her needs were supplied. I know that I may have not been there for emotional support, but it was not from a lack of trying on my part. She pushed me further and further away the older she got. Part of me just wanted to give up, but I knew that the DuBois Curse would and could not win.

I went back to work and found out that while I was gone, Jake had fired some older dancers and hired some new dancers. Jake had stopped hiring dancers long ago. I confronted Jake about his decision to fire and hire when I was gone and he said, "Look, we need some fresh meat on stage. Some of these dancers are just old and burnt out."

I was surprised to hear Jake speak that way about the dancers. They all were so loyal to him and The Club. Yes, there were some that had been there for a long time, but not much longer than I had.

"So Jake, are you telling me I am a tired dancer now?"

"No, Mystery, I am not talking about you. You got something special. Those other tired-ass women are just broke down. They don't excite our clients like they did back in the day. And the reason we have so many people Thursday through Saturday is because of what you have done. They are not coming here for the dancers. This is a strip joint and our main attraction should be the dancers. We gotta step it up if we wanna remain on top."

I was upset because new girls required training. I trained all of the dancers and I was not up to training four new girls at one time.

One of the girls, Chardonnay, had a serious attitude. She was probably about two years older than me and could stop men in their tracks with her looks. When it came to dancing, she thought that she was the best and that no one could teach her anything that she did not already know. Before I knew it, Chardonnay was acting as if she was running The Club. I found out that she was even soliciting some of my Private Room clients. I confronted her about it and she told me The Club would run better if there was new blood. She went on to say that my time at The Club was over.

As long as I had been at The Club, I had never gotten into a physical confrontation with anyone. Before I realized it, I had slapped Chardonnay and we were rumbling around in the dancers' dressing room. I had Chardonnay pinned up against one of the mirrors and was banging her head on the mirror until I noticed blood dripping form her forehead. Once I saw blood, I backed off, but I had already knocked her unconscious.

Someone must have called the ambulance and the police because before I realized it, I was being handcuffed and put into a police car. I was taken down to the station where Lieutenant Prince, who I knew intimately, told them to uncuff me so he could speak with me.

"Mystery, what the hell happened?"

"I don't know, Prince. I just snapped. That bitch said the wrong thing at the wrong time."

"What happened was that she pulled a knife on you and you were protecting yourself. I think when she was rushed to the hospital they found a 6 inch blade on her," said Lieutenant Prince.

"Okay, so what are you going to do with me?"

"I am going to have to book you so it will look like we are trying to do our job. But I will get a judge involved so we can let you out on your own recognizance based on the story that you have told us and the fact that you have a clean arrest record."

"I can't spend a night in jail, Prince!"

"Who said you would be in a cell? I am sure it is something that we can work out," he said, smiling. "My detective will question you and you make certain you say it was self-defense and I will take care of the rest," Prince said.

I did as Prince told me to do when questioned by the detective. I was about to be booked into custody when another officer came to the door and asked to speak to the detective. The detective came back and told me that I had lucked out. He told me that Chardonnay had regained consciousness and insisted that she did not want to press any charges. He then attempted to flirt and I quickly rejected him so he said, "Okay. You are free to go."

I immediately called Jake, who was already at The Club. The girls had apparently filled him in on what had happened. He told me to take the night off and that he would speak to me tomorrow. I was getting off the phone when I noticed the handsome, quiet guy who always came to see me strip on Wednesdays leaving the police station. I had always wanted to say something to him because he would leave me no less than $400 each time he came. But I did not know whether to speak to him or run, since I had barely escaped an arrest.

He looked directly at me and said, "You must have been arrested for stealing."

"Stealing?" I asked.

"Yeah, stealing someone's heart, because you have truly stolen mine."

"No. I have been arrested for a TKO. So you better watch out."

"I am not afraid. My brother is the lieutenant here."

"Prince?"

"Oh no, you must be a regular criminal! You are on a first name basis?"

"No, not regular, just an intermittent criminal." I loved all of the words I was learning to use.

"Well, Mystery, maybe I can lead you into living a more legal life by spending time with me."

"Now I am feeling at a disadvantage. You know my name, where I work, and where I sometimes visit. But I know nothing about you."

"Well, come on. Join me for drinks and I will fill you in."

I normally would have rejected him, but I always wondered about the man who left me so much money every Wednesday. I agreed to join him.

We went to my favorite restaurant, Pappadeaux's. We sat and talked for hours. Before we knew it, the restaurant was empty and we were the last patrons, but we did not actually leave until someone started flickering the lights.

He looked at me and said, "I am ready to begin the rest of our lives."

I looked at him and laughed and told him that patience is a virtue.

Chapter 9

My big tipper's name was Dr. Emmit Little. Unlike Kwame, he was a real doctor who worked at a hospital. He explained that he was a cardiologist, which in the past I had just referred to as a heart doctor. I was confused about Lieutenant Prince and Dr. Little being brothers, but he explained that they had the same mother, but different fathers. He explained that Prince's father was physically abusive to his mother and Prince. She ran away to a shelter, where she ended up marrying the shelter's manager, Emmit's dad. Emmit's dad raised Prince as if he was his own child, and their parents had been happily married for thirty-two years.

Emmit inquired as to how I knew Prince, but I made up some story about meeting him based on problems we used to have at The Club. Emmit looked up to Prince so much that I did not have the heart to tell him that Prince frequented The Club and was one of my favorite Private Room clients. I was more interested in why a nice-looking doctor would come to a strip club every week and drop hundreds on a stripper he did not know. When I asked Emmit why he came almost every Wednesday, he told me the first time he came it was with a group of guys for a bachelor party. He saw me and it was love at first sight. He then came back each week, trying to get enough nerve to ask me out.

I knew that I was not going to introduce Emmit to Aunt Hattie or Porchia until I knew that he was right for me. He seemed to be innocent enough and he came from a household with two parents. I did not know many people whose parents were together for thirty years and as happy as Emmit portrayed his family to be. I knew that his brother was not happily married since he spent so much time in the Private Room - or maybe the Private Room is what kept his marriage happy. I viewed a happy marriage as a husband and wife being faithful to each other while truly enjoying each other's company. I don't know if such a thing existed, but that is how I pictured a happy marriage.

The Club was not a place that I took much enjoyment in anymore. Chardonnay came back to The Club despite my objections to Jake. The word on the street was that Jake and Chardonnay were a couple. She used everything she could to gain favor from him. Jake and I had arguments that we never had prior to her coming to The Club. She evidently had been filling his head with information on how she felt The Club should be run. It started taking a toll on our dancers. There were some that wanted to be loyal to me, while others wanted to be loyal to Chardonnay. I called Big

John to let him know that I was going to leave The Club.

Big John pulled Jake and me together for a meeting. He presented the idea of opening another club and letting me be the sole manager for his new club. He said that he would pay me a salary and I would earn 30% of the sales from the new club. I jumped at the opportunity to start a new venture. After all, this would give me the experience I needed to be able to open my own club. I had completed my certificate program and was anxious to put all my learnings to work. Jake seemed to be happy about the new arrangement, but something told me that he was not as supportive as he pretended.

I shared what I was doing with Aunt Hattie and she was very excited. Aunt Hattie had a lot of admiration for my grandmother and she said, "Mystery, you have your grandmother's skills."

All I could think about was that my grandmother was a despicable person. How could a mother pimp out her own underage daughter? I did not share the same admiration for my grandmother as Aunt Hattie did, and I told Aunt Hattie that I did not appreciate her comparing me to my grandmother.

I did everything to avoid Emmit and discourage him from pursuing me. I did not feel that we were, as the Bible states, equally yoked. We had very different upbringings, and he did not understand much about living life in the hood. Although I enjoyed our conversations, I liked men that had book smarts, along with a lot of street sense. Frankly, I found Emmit to be a little too square and me to be a little too street.

However, he continued to come to The Club when I was stripping on Wednesdays. When I pulled away from The Club to work on opening BJ's Playground, he called me and asked me out several times. I gave him the excuse that I was too busy trying to open up a new club. On opening night, Emmit was the first one present to check out the new venue.

My concept for BJ's Playground was a little different than The Club. It was more of an entertainment venue. We did not have dancers stripping in the main room, but we had a room designated for those interested in strippers. I eliminated the Private Room because that is where most of the prostitution took place. I thought about how Porchia would always talk about me being a ho and yes, we did ho from the Private Room.

The dancers at BJ's Playground worked strictly for tips without the extracurricular activities. BJ's Playground was open from Wednesday through Sunday and hosted a variety of events, including showcases for new comedians, local musicians, jam sessions, and spoken word. Emmit waited for me to close up after the first night with two dozen red velvet roses. He told me that he knew that I would make BJ's Playground successful, but that he would miss watching me dance.

I was feeling great because opening night was a success. Emmit told me he would love to take me to dinner, but most respectable establishments were closed at that time in the morning. He asked me to go with him to his house and told me that he would prepare a celebration meal. I still felt that Emmit was not the right man for me, but I agreed to the celebration dinner.

Emmit lived in Fannin Station in a tri-level four-bedroom house near the Medical Center. It was a rather modest place for a cardiologist, but Emmit said he was a self-proclaimed minimalist. I was not certain what a minimalist was, but he really did not know how to decorate. He had only the essentials like a table to eat, a sofa to sit on, and a bed to sleep in. There was absolutely no decoration, paintings, or artwork within his place. I noticed that he did not have a television or stereo either.

"So Doctor, what do you do in your spare time?"

"Think about you."

"I am serious. You have no form of entertainment in here."

"Mystery, I work a lot. In addition to my practice, I also teach at U of H. I don't have much time for entertainment. I really looked forward to going to see you dance on Wednesdays. That is really my only day off. I am usually working or preparing for classes on the days that I am not at the hospital."

I walked over toward his office and saw that he had both a laptop and desktop. "Well, I am glad you do have a computer. Otherwise I would think you were a caveman."

"Well, I would live any way that you wanted me to live if you were my lady."

I ignored his comment and asked him, "So do you ever take vacations?"

"I don't have anyone to take a vacation with," he answered. He walked over with a glass of red wine and said, "I want to toast you being a very beautiful, clever, ambitious, sexy woman."

"I will toast to that, Doctor," I said as we clicked glasses. "Emmit, what do you want for the rest of your life?"

"I want what every other American desires: a loving wife with 2.1 children, a dog, and a house with a white picket fence. What do you want, Mystery?"

"To be happy," I answered.

He cuddled up close to me and said, "I would love to make you happy."

I pulled away and said, "We may have different ideas of happiness."

"Hold that thought," Emmit said. "I want to get our dinner ready."

Emmit made tasty seafood pasta with pesto sauce, a green salad, mixed vegetables, and bread. I thought to myself, *Ooh, is this what Baby Face was singing about when he made the song "As Soon as I Get Home"?* We actually had great conversation about his childhood and the things that they did as a family. It was so unlike my childhood; I could not relate too much to what he was saying. When he asked me about my childhood, I told him my mother died when I was young and that I did not have much of a childhood. I thought that was the most honest I could be with him at the time.

By the end of the night, I was in his bed and I heard fireworks go off as we made love. This man must have put the "L" in lovemaking. He took me to a place that I had never been before and was not sure I ever wanted to go again, unless it was forever. I was lost in pure ecstasy for hours. He made love to everything from my fingers to my toes. He told me he had dreamt many times about the things he wanted to do to me if he ever had the opportunity. I am sure he did that and much more. By the time I left Emmit, I had lost all sense of reality and I thought just being in bed with him for the rest of my life would make me happy.

I snapped back to reality when Porchia called as I was driving away.

"Mystery, where are you?" asked Porchia.

"On my way home. Why?"

"Aunt Hattie is having bad heartburn. Can you bring home some Maalox?"

"I am not certain where I will find Maalox at this hour, but I will do my best," I responded.

"Well, do the best you can 'cause she is in a lot of pain."

"Okay. I will see you soon."

When I arrived home, Porchia and Aunt Hattie were waiting on me. Aunt Hattie looked like she had eaten too many hot peppers. I quickly handed her the medicine and she said over and over, "Thank you, Lord." After the third, "thank you, Lord", Porchia told

Aunt Hattie that the Lord did not bring her anything, but I had.

Aunt Hattie responded, "Baby Girl, Mystery was only the vehicle for what the Lord has done. Nobody can do you like Jesus."

Porchia looked at Aunt Hattie with a smirk and said, "Aunt Hattie, if Jesus was all that, He would have his own car and bring you what you need."

Aunt Hattie replied, "Go on girl, get out of my face!"

Porchia kissed Aunt Hattie and left.

This gave me an opportunity to speak with Aunt Hattie about her constant heartburn. "Aunt Hattie, we probably should go get you checked out," I said.

"Mystery, I am fine. Baby, you worry too much."

"Well, I am going to set you up an appointment just to make sure."

"Make yourself happy, girl. But I told you that I am okay."

I called Emmit to tell him about Aunt Hattie. He agreed to see her and make certain everything was okay.

Chapter 10

Although Aunt Hattie agreed to go see a doctor, she came up with an excuse each time I would bring it up. Emmit gave me advice on what to do to help Aunt Hattie, including taking aspirin on a daily basis. I spent a lot of time away from the house so I could only make certain she was doing things when I was there. She insisted on not letting Porchia know about anything that did not involve school. I agreed with that, but I also just wished I could be at home more to help Aunt Hattie.

Since I was the only manager, BJ's Playground took me away from home more than I liked. Emmit and I saw each other between our busy schedules. Since Wednesday was his down day, I met him at his house quite often for an afternoon tune-up. I gave up my massages for our Wednesday rendezvous. I could not take Emmit seriously because I still did not understand what he saw in me. I was content with having fantastic sex with a cool dude.

Porchia became unbearable by the time she entered 11th grade. I loved her, but I could not stand her. We argued about everything. We argued about her keeping her room clean. We argued about the bathroom. We argued about her spending too much time with Chanti and Tracy. We argued about her not focusing enough on school. I don't think we had a decent conversation in two years. She did not care about anything but basketball, school, her girls, and Aunt Hattie.

One Sunday I was getting ready to take a shower so Aunt Hattie and I could go to Sunday school. Porchia had clothes sprawled all over the bathroom. I literally could not get into the shower. I asked her to get all of her clothes out so I could take a shower. That devil child stormed into the bathroom and pushed me into the bathtub. I was ready to get up and beat the daylights out of her. Aunt Hattie came and broke it up before anything could happen. Aunt Hattie followed Porchia into her room and the next thing I knew Porchia was shouting for me to call 911.

After calling 911, I called Emmit to let him know that Aunt Hattie had suffered what we thought was a heart attack. He asked me where were they taking her and I told him that the paramedics said they were taking her to General. Emmit told me he would see what he could do. When we arrived at General, we were told that Aunt Hattie had been taken to Memorial. I was relieved, knowing that Emmit was on duty at Memorial. I knew he would do everything he could to make certain Aunt Hattie was properly taken care of.

If it was not enough that I had to deal with almost losing Aunt Hattie, I found out that Porchia was dating some thug drug dealer. He was probably about Porchia's age and he drove a brand new Benz. When I asked him whether he was a drug dealer, he said he did not sell drugs, but no one in the hood rolled like that at his age without being involved in illegal activities. I was so afraid that I would lose Porchia. Although she might not be a ho, I was afraid I would lose her to drugs or an early pregnancy. I feared that the DuBois Curse could not be broken.

After arriving at Memorial, I found out that Emmit was responsible for having Aunt Hattie transferred from General to Memorial so he could have direct supervision over the surgery and serve as her doctor. After surgery, Emmit came in with a look on his face that made me think we had lost her. I was so happy when he told us that she was recuperating. I asked Emmit to act as if he did not know me because I needed time to introduce him to my aunt and my cousin. He agreed to go along with my request for a little while, but he insisted that we needed to be honest with them. According to Emmit, honesty was the best virtue that a person could have.

I did not want to introduce him to Aunt Hattie or Porchia unless I knew that we were in a serious, committed relationship. I did not tell Emmit about Porchia because I could not risk this information getting back to her. The only thing I knew we were both committed to was having sex on Wednesdays. Although he spoke about us being together forever, I assumed this was only pillow talk. Frankly, I was happy with our arrangement because much of my time needed to be dedicated to running BJ's Playground.

While Emmit took good care of Aunt Hattie, he also took good care of me. I stayed around the hospital during Aunt Hattie's recovery. Emmit and I took advantage of this time to find the best places to make love. We had sex in a vacant operating room, the medicine storage closet, the stairwell, the conference room, an empty patient's room, and on his desktop. We kept the Ms. Dubois-Dr. Little charade going until Porchia ran into his office and caught me giving him head.

After Porchia found us in Emmit's office, it destroyed the already bad relationship I had with Porchia. She took every chance to disrespect me any time we were present in the same room. She let everyone know that she thought I was the biggest tramp in H-town. Unlike when she was a little girl and embarrassed about what people said about me, she would now do or say anything to let people know that although we were cousins, she was nothing like me. I hurt every time she did something evil or said something nasty. But my skin grew thicker with each time because I knew it was only the DuBois Curse trying to win again.

Not everything was bad as it related to Porchia. My girl received scholarship offers from several schools. She was excelling in basketball and in all of her subjects at school. As time passed, she also seemed to warm up to Emmit. He was growing on me too. So what if he was not street smart? He did everything to make me happy. Even more important to me, he accepted me for who I was and not who he wanted me to be. Aunt Hattie was also well on the road to recovery with assistance from Emmit and Porchia's boyfriend, Tyrese Gamble. That boy that I thought was a drug-dealing thug was actually a professional basketball player. I was really surprised that he paid for Aunt Hattie to have a full-time nurse to help her through her recovery period.

Although I was happy that Ty was not a drug dealer, I was concerned that he might get Porchia side-tracked. She spoke about being a research scientist who would find a cure for cancer. I did not want her to become so wrapped up in Ty that she gave up on her dreams or became a teenage mother like me. Every time I would bring up the subject of sex, she would tell me that I was overqualified to give her advice. I guess that was just another way of her calling me a ho.

One day Porchia left her phone laying on the kitchen table while she went into the bathroom. I took her phone and scrolled the list, looking for Ty's number. Most of the numbers on her phone were local phone numbers. I saw a lot of "Unknown" calls but did not see anything that said Ty or Tyrese.

Aunt Hattie's nurse was being paid by Ty so I thought she might know the number. I approached her and told her I needed to discuss the arrangements for her service with Ty and asked her if she might have the number. I was so happy when she produced the number without any further questions.

I called Ty the next day to have a conversation with him about Porchia since she was unwilling to discuss their relationship.

He answered, "Hello?"

"Hello. Is this Ty?"

"Who is this?" asked Ty.

"Hi Ty, this is Mystery?"

"Hey, Mystery. Is everything okay?"

"Yes. Ty, I need to talk with you, but I need your word that everything we talk about will be kept in confidence. You can't let Porchia know that I called you or tell her what we spoke about."

"I am not sure I am comfortable with that. Depends on what you have to say."

"It has to do with making sure Porchia succeeds in what she needs to do."

"I am definitely supportive of that, Mystery."

"Porchia had dreams of going to college before she met you."

"I am not aware that any of that has changed," said Ty.

"I just want to make sure it doesn't."

"We are on the same team - Team Porchia," he said.

"Look, Ty, I don't know if you two or having sex, but please be safe. I hope you wear protection at all times."

"I won't do anything to prevent Porchia from reaching her goals, Mystery."

"Okay, cool. We are on the same page. So our conversation is between us, right?" I asked.

"I will not mention this conversation to Porchia. You know, I think it is great that you take such interest in her. She is lucky to have a cousin like you."

"I am blessed to have her, Ty."

"My exact feelings too, Mystery. I only want what's best for her and will do anything to support her dreams and desires in any way that I can."

"Thanks, Ty."

"No problem. I need to run. Take care of my girl while I'm gone."

I wanted to say what the hell do you think I have been doing for the last seventeen years? But instead I just said, "See you soon."

Chapter 11

Just when the sun seems like it will shine forever, the rain starts to pour. Aunt Hattie says that problems are good because as believers, it makes us stronger in our faith in God. I say a little rain is fine, but a storm is too much.

I saw my daughter almost fall apart when her best friend, Chanti, was killed. I did not know what to say or what to do to comfort her. If that was not bad enough, she also found Cherelle dead in their house.

I would have done anything to take her pain away. Porchia was always so spunky, but during this period, she became withdrawn. The only person who seemed to help was Ty. Although he was busy with playing basketball, he would come around when he thought Porchia needed him. He surprised her at Chanti's and Cherelle's funeral. It was then that I realized that the boy must really love Porchia.

I was going through problems of my own during this time. Some female had been leaving threatening voicemails at BJ's Playground. In the first message, she said, "Bitch, you gonna find out that your shit stank!" The second message said, "Watch your back." The third message said, "Bitch, you are done!" After the third message I mentioned it to Emmit and he told me I should contact his brother.

I did not take the threats seriously because I thought it may have been Chardonnay.

Word out in the Ward was that The Club was no longer doing well financially and that Big John was either going to sell it or close it down. I did not speak to Big John much those days because he was going through emotional issues due to Cherelle's and Chanti's deaths. I thought the best way to help him was by me keeping BJ's Playground profitable.

About 4 a.m., I received a call from Big John to meet him at BJ's immediately.

"What's wrong?" I asked, trying to wake up from my thirty minutes of sound sleep.

"Just hurry," said Big John and then he ended the call.

I frantically scrambled around to find something to put on to run out to BJ's. When I arrived, the firefighters were still trying to put out the fire. Right before my eyes, all my dedication, time, and effort had gone up in smoke. I looked at Big John and he was just blankly staring at the blaze.

"Big John, I am so sorry," I said with tears in my eyes.

Big John looked at me then gave me a hug and said, "No, Moneymaker, I am sorry. I know this was your baby."

Big John started calling me Moneymaker after my first year working at The Club because he said I was the reason The Club was a success. We stood embracing until the firefighter came over and said, "We have done what we can. It's a total loss."

I called Emmit to tell him about the fire and he told me he was on his way to pick me up. I told him that I would drive over to his house. Porchia had gone on a school tour so I called to check on Aunt Hattie. I told her what happened and that I would probably be out most of the night.

I drove over to Emmit's house and within the first thirty minutes of being in bed with him, I forgot about BJ's Playground. I did not know what it was about that man, but he made every inch of my body feel good. It was as if he got pleasure from pleasing me, which turned me on even more. I woke up to a sunny room and Emmit staring at me.

"Good Morning, Sunshine," Emmit said.

"Good Morning. How long have you been staring at me?"

"Not long enough. You are so beautiful."

"Wow! A girl could get used to this," I said while scooting closer to him.

"So did you sleep well?" asked Emmit.

"Better than I have in a few months."

"Well, perhaps it is time for you to rest," Emmit said.

Everything that happened the previous night came rushing back to me at once. "Rest? I can't rest. I have to figure out my next move. I have no job."

"Mystery, you have been working hard. There is nothing wrong with resting. I would not mind taking care of you."

"What do you mean you would not mind taking care of me?"

"I would take care of you physically, mentally, financially, or any other way you would like me to take care of you."

"Yeah, I like the way you take care of me physically," I said while kissing him on his neck.

"Mystery, I am serious. I would like to take care of you."

I pulled away from him and said, "I don't need you to take care of me. I have taken care of myself for twenty-eight years and I don't need anyone to take care of me now."

"I know that you can take care of yourself. That is what I love about you. But there is nothing wrong with someone wanting to take care of you."

"I am not a possession, Emmit. You are speaking like I am an object or a child. I am a grown-ass woman."

"I am well aware that you are a grown woman. Perhaps this is not the time to talk about it."

"I need to get home. I know Aunt Hattie is probably worried about me."

I got up and went to his bathroom to freshen up and dress. When I came out of the bathroom, he was in the kitchen making coffee with only his shorts and slippers on. *Dang, that man is fine!* I looked at him and wanted to get back in bed, but I knew Aunt Hattie was waiting for me to take her to church. When I looked at Emmit he looked so broken. I walked up to him and said, "I can't stay for coffee, but I can see you tonight."

He looked at me and said, "I am sorry. I need to prepare for classes."

I snatched up my purse, walked out, looked back, and said, "Your loss."

As I drove home I was trying to figure out what that fight was about. I had cut off the man's head for him saying that he wanted to take care of me. I felt like he was treating me like I was a ho. In exchange for good sex, he would take care of me. I did not want that from him or any man. Despite what Porchia thought, I ain't nobody's ho. I knew Emmit was a good man, but unless he treated me like someone that he wanted to be with for the rest of his life, I was ready to move on.

I tried to sneak into the house so as not to catch any slack from Aunt Hattie for being out all night, but she was sitting and waiting for me in her chair when I walked in.

"Well, I see you finally decided to come home."

"Yes. I am sorry I stayed out longer than I thought, but I came back in time for church. Why are you not getting ready?"

"Baby, I am taking time to reflect and pray."

"What's wrong, Aunt Hattie? Is it your heart!"

"No, baby. It is not that. It is the anniversary of your grandmother's death. Around this time every year I feel a little down."

"Aunt Hattie, you always talk about my grandmother like she was some type of hero. She ran a ho house. She pimped out her daughter when she was a child. She should be horrified, not glorified!"

"Baby, your grandmother and God are the reasons I am alive. I never told you that she took a bullet for me."

"What are you talking about, Aunt Hattie?"

"I upset one of the johns because I refused to let him back in the house. He enjoyed doing crazy things to the girls. He wanted to tie them up and torture them. That is not the type of house we ran. Well, he was about to shoot me, and your grandmother came out and told him that he would have to come through her first. And that is exactly what he did. He shot her right there before my own eyes."

"What?"

"I also never told you that we were lovers."

"What!" I exclaimed.

"Let me finish, baby. I did not know she was pimping out your mother. When I found out, I stepped in and stopped it."

"Aunt Hattie, you are a lesbian!"

"Girl, I have told you all of that and the only question you have for me is whether I am a lesbian?"

"I am in shock. I never even suspected."

"I was lost after your grandmother was killed. I began doing drugs to ease the pain. Once I started, I became lost in it, so lost that one day I overdosed. My heart completely stopped and I was pronounced dead on the scene. They covered my body with a sheet and was about to take me away when one of the EMTs told them he thought he saw me breathe."

"Aunt Hattie, you were not dead?

"Yes I was, child. But God not only revived me, He washed away all of my sins. Ever since that day I have been walking hand in hand with Him. That is why I always say that can't nobody do you like Jesus. But sometimes I wonder, if your grandmother would not have taken that bullet, where would I be today? I feel that I was saved twice, once by your grandmother and once by the grace of God."

I got up and hugged Aunt Hattie and told her that I loved her. I had no idea what she had been through. I now understood why she always brought up my grandmother. I started thinking perhaps Aunt Hattie was put in my life to make sure the DuBois Curse was broken. She had always been a part of my life as long as I could remember. She was never damning, but always a very comforting, loving woman. It was at that time I realized that Porchia and I were blessed to have such a strong woman as our role model.

Chapter 12

I always felt that people were either good or bad-natured, and no one could make a good person bad; although I always believed that a good person can make a bad person better. I found out the hard way that this was not true.

The investigators discovered that Jake and Chardonnay were responsible for burning down the club because they felt that BJ's Playground had taken all of their clients away. They were both arrested and convicted of arson and each of them was sentenced to twenty years in prison and ordered to pay a $10,000 fine. After that revelation, Big John decided to get out of the adult entertainment business. He had several other legal and profitable businesses that would keep him afloat for the rest of his life. He also told me that if I ever needed anything, he was only a phone call away.

On the other hand, Ms. Carletta was a good woman who could not change Duke. Instead of Duke getting better, Ms. Carletta turned into a killer. Ms. Carletta killed Duke for molesting Tracy. The good news was that Ms. Carletta only spent a week in jail for killing

Duke, and his death made my dreams come alive. Porchia would be able to cash in on her insurance policy for school, and I would be able to use the money I saved toward opening up my own business.

The most difficult part was having to tell Porchia that the man she detested was her father. I spoke with Aunt Hattie about it and her advice was, "Baby, the truth shall set you free."

That might be true, but it also might set the Dubois Curse free. I knew that she despised that man, but she would probably not be able to forgive us for not telling her. I also did not think that she would ever forgive me for not letting her know that I was her mother, or that Tracy was her sister. I was willing to take this information to the grave if I could figure out a way to cash in on Porchia's insurance policy without her knowledge.

I contacted a former client from The Club who was in the insurance business to ask about how insurance policies worked for children. He told me that if a person was a minor and there was no one listed as guardian on the policy, the parent or legal guardian could go to court to ask to be the guardian of the funds. I decided I did not want to go to court because the information that I am Porchia's mother would then be public information. Porchia was going to be eighteen in less than a year, so she would be entitled to all of her money. Once Porchia turned eighteen, we could tell her that Duke was her father, but maintain the story that her mother died from cancer.

Aunt Hattie kept close contact on what was going on at Porchia's school. One afternoon she decided to call her friend, Joel Ashton, the principal, to check in on Porchia. She had not revealed a lot of what had been happening at school. Aunt Hattie hung up the phone and starting screaming.

"What is going on, Aunt Hattie?"

"Hallelujah! Thank you Jesus."

"Don't keep me wondering, Aunt Hattie."

"Baby Girl is going to graduate early and go to D.C. for college."

"What?"

"Yes, baby, and they are going to pay her to go."

"You mean she got a scholarship?" I asked.

"Yes. They are going to pay for everything."

I started screaming while Aunt Hattie began thanking Jesus again. "Brother Ashton asked us to let Porchia tell us her good news," said Aunt Hattie.

"This is reason to celebrate! We should go out for dinner," I said.

"Mystery, did you hear me? We have to let Baby Girl tell us."

"Okay, Aunt Hattie. Let us go celebrate! I want to take you out to dinner."

"Can we go to Piccadilly?" asked Aunt Hattie.

I did not want to go to Piccadilly, but that was one of Aunt Hattie's favorite places so I said, "Sure, anywhere you want to go."

When Aunt Hattie and I arrived back home, Emmit called me and said he was coming over to check on

Aunt Hattie. I was so excited! I could not wait for him to arrive and I told him about Porchia's offer. He sounded a little disappointed and asked what had happened to Stanford. He was visiting Aunt Hattie when Porchia received an offer to attend Stanford, the school he attended for his undergraduate degree. But we all knew that Stanford was Porchia's second choice. Her first choice was Georgetown University. I was just happy for her to be getting a scholarship. This gave me the time I needed to figure out how to tell Porchia about her life insurance policy.

Emmit came over with the biggest smile on his face. "Hello, Sunshine. You are looking beautiful, as usual."

"So why are you so happy today?"

"Aren't I always happy?

"Yes, but you have sparkles in your eyes today."

"I am happy to see you, Mystery," he said, pulling me close to him and kissing me.

I was surprised by this move because we were still keeping our relationship under wraps.

"So where is my favorite patient?" he asked.

"She is getting all pretty for you. You know she is a flirt."

Emmit laughed and said, "So you got it honestly."

Aunt Hattie came out looking better than she did for our Piccadilly date. "Hello, Doctor. To what do I owe this pleasure?" asked Aunt Hattie.

Emmit went over to Aunt Hattie and kissed her on the cheeks and said, "You know I have to check on my favorite patient. So how are you feeling?"

"Like I am twenty-one years old."

Emmit laughed and said, "Well, you are looking like you are eighteen years old."

Aunt Hattie laughed and said, "Now Doctor, why are you always coming on to me? Have a seat, please."

"Thank you." Emmit sat on the sofa and grabbed my hand, to my surprise, to sit on the side of him. Aunt Hattie sat in her chair with a confused look on her face. "Ms. Hattie, I came here to see you, but I have another reason for being here."

"Yes? What is it, Doctor?" asked Aunt Hattie.

Emmit looked at me then back at Aunt Hattie and said, "I have come here to ask you for Mystery's hand in marriage."

"What did you say?" I asked.

"I have come here to ask your aunt if it is okay with her if we get married," Emmit repeated.

"Now I knew you too were sneaking around, but I never thought this," said Aunt Hattie.

"Aunt Hattie!" I shouted.

"Yes, Mystery. I was born one day, but not yesterday. Now what makes you want to marry Mystery, Doctor?" asked Aunt Hattie.

"Simply saying that I love her does not reflect how she makes me feel. I feel alive. I feel that I can do anything. She makes me feel whole."

Aunt Hattie interrupted him and said, "You know Jesus does the same thing."

"Ms. Hattie, I am familiar with Jesus. The Bible also says that he who finds a wife finds a good thing. And Mystery is definitely my good thing."

"And son, do you understand Ephesians 5:22-33 that says, 'Wives, submit to your own husbands, as to the Lord. For the husband is the head of the wife even as Christ is the head of the church, his body, and is himself its Savior. Now as the church submits to Christ, so also wives should submit in everything to their husbands. Husbands, love your wives, as Christ loved the church and gave himself up for her, that he might sanctify her, having cleansed her by the washing of water with the word," Aunt Hattie said without taking a breath.

"Yes ma'am, I do," responded Emmit.

"The Bible gives you both responsibility. But do you know what love is?" asked Aunt Hattie.

"What do you mean, Ms. Hattie?"

"The Bible also helps you with that. The Bible tells us that love is patient and kind. Love does not envy or boast. It is not arrogant or rude. It does not insist on its own way. It is not irritable or resentful. It does not rejoice at wrongdoing, but rejoices with the truth. Love bears all things, believes all things, hopes all things, and endures all things. Do you understand that, son?"

"Yes, Ms. Hattie, I do."

"Well, it is not up to me, but up to her if she chooses to marry you."

I could not believe that Aunt Hattie had taken Emmit through a whole sermon to tell him that it was not up to her. After Aunt Hattie finished her sermon, Emmit took a box out of his pocket, got on his knees, took out a ring, and said, "Mystery DuBois, will you marry me?"

I shouted, "Yes! Yes! Yes!"

Aunt Hattie got up and congratulated us both and said, "This is cause for another celebration. Come on, let's go to the kitchen for some of my peach cobbler and coffee."

"Ms. Hattie, I hope that is a sugarless peach cobbler made with wheat flour."

"Son, you need to take off your doctor hat and put on your aunt-in-law hat and keep yo' mouth shut."

Emmit laughed and said, "Yes, ma'am."

When Emmit left I really started celebrating. I could not believe the size of the diamond. It was humongous. I felt like I might get jacked wearing this around in the Ward. Aunt Hattie seemed a little reserved about the proposal, but she insisted that she was happy for me. I was doing my happy dance when Porchia walked into the kitchen.

She looked at us and asked what was going on, and I told her that I was marrying Dr. Little. Instead of congratulating me, she made a snide comment about me ho'in' to get him. I lost it. I had allowed her to disrespect me for years, but on the happiest day of my life since her birth, I would not take any more abuse. I yelled and told her that she was the most ungrateful, cruel person I had ever met.

Aunt Hattie jumped in to stop the fight by pretending her heart was hurting. My heart was really hurting. That is when I realized that anything that I did for that child would never be enough.

Chapter 13

Emmit gave me a $30,000 budget to start planning our wedding. We also decided to build a house in Sugarland, Texas, which was a suburb of Houston. I suddenly became very busy with wedding planners, architects, and general contractors. Emmit made it clear to me that he would be available for advice, but both the wedding and the home were my projects. It was also clear that Emmit did not want me to work in any fashion outside of catering to our home and family needs. We discussed that Aunt Hattie would live with us once the house was built.

It seemed much easier to work on the house than it was to plan our wedding. Emmit had three people to stand with him at the wedding, and I had none. Emmit was going to have his brother as his best man. One of his groomsmen was going to be a fellow doctor from work, and the other, his best friend from his early childhood while growing up. There were only two women in my life: Aunt Hattie and Porchia. One was too old to be a bridesmaid and the other one hated me.

I asked Prince's wife to be one of my bridesmaids. Emmit introduced me to Rebecca who, to my surprise, was white. Now I knew why Prince spent a lot of time in the Private Room. He missed having sex with a sistah. Prince and I also had a discussion where we both decided it was best to never tell Emmit about our Private Room relationship. I was still short a maid of honor and one bridesmaid. I asked one of the girls, Jess, who worked for me at BJ's Playground. She was one of my favorite dancers and she was very happy that I asked her to be one of my bridesmaids.

Aunt Hattie convinced me to ask Porchia to be my maid of honor. I prepared myself to suck up all of my pride and ready myself for any abuse she might dish out as a result of me asking her to stand in my wedding. I picked her up from the airport from a visit with Ty and I was surprised that when I asked her, she did not react in her usual fashion. I was ready for her to call me names and cuss me out. Instead, she was silent. I did not know if this was hope for our relationship, or just Porchia's bliss from being with Ty.

Now that I had all of my bridesmaids, I could begin preparing for my wedding. I found a wedding consultant to help me flesh out my ideas. He was highly rated on Yelp so I felt confident that together we could plan a perfect wedding for me and my perfect fiancé. He met me at the house and presented several exceptional ideas. I opted for a vintage wedding that included everything from a vintage car to vintage gowns. I spoke with Emmit and he loved the idea. I thought it was great how he thought everything I did was wonderful, unlike Porchia, who thought I was a walking disaster. He felt that the moment I woke up, everything would be right in his world.

The plans for the house were also coming along. Our dream home would be an eight bedroom, ten bathroom house. Emmit thought that was way too many bathrooms, but all of the bedrooms had a bathroom and there was also a bathroom off the kitchen and another one off the entertaining room. All I could think about was how I grew up most of my life sharing a bathroom with Aunt Hattie and Porchia. As Porchia grew older, it became more difficult for the three of us. There were too many times one of us stood at the door waiting for someone else to come out. I would go down fighting to have enough bathrooms in my dream house.

My wedding consultant, Jaime, arranged for me to go pick out wedding dresses at a boutique located downtown. I walked in excited, and there was Chardonnay standing there looking as if she owned the store. Chardonnay was supposed to still be in jail!

She walked over to me and said, "So are you shopping for your treasure chest?"

I thought to myself, *This bitch is about to get beat down!* She had burnt down my place, caused me to lose my job, yet she was prancing around like she was Mother Theresa reincarnated. Then I remembered that I was marrying the man of my dreams while she was working at a wedding boutique.

"Hi, Chardonnay. So did you learn a new skill while you were in the pen?"

"Never really served any time. I had an attorney who got me out on a technicality."

"And where is your boyfriend?"

"My boyfriend owns this store, and I am the manager."

"Jake owns this store?"

"No, Jake is in jail."

This ho was out and Jake was in jail! Whoever said justice is blind was blind.

"So what do you need, Mystery?" asked Chardonnay.

"Nothing from you, bitch," I responded and then walked away.

When I got to my car, I called Jaime.

"Hi, Jaime, this is Ms. DuBois."

"Well hello, darling. Did you find your experience at the boutique absolutely fabulous? Isn't Chardonnay a doll? And I bet you found the most marvelous dress."

"No, darling. We need to find another boutique."

"Why? What happened?"

"Chardonnay was rude and she is a well-known criminal. You really need to be careful about who you associate with."

"I beg your pardon?"

"Yes, darling, she is a criminal."

"Well, Ms. DuBois, I am sure I can find someone else for you."

"Don't bother, Jaime. I will find a more conscientious wedding planner."

I knew that Jaime did not like being called a wedding planner. When I first met him, he made certain he proclaimed that he was not a wedding planner, but a wedding consultant. He brought dreams to reality. Well, this was starting off as a nightmare.

"I am so sorry, Ms. DuBois."

"You should be," I said as I hung up the phone.

I was upset because I really liked Jaime. Now I had the job of trying to find another wedding planner.

Aunt Hattie came up with a name of a lady who was from the Ward. I met with her and told of her about my ideas. She was nowhere near as trendy as Jaime, but I somehow knew she would be able to pull it off. Shareese convinced me that I would be able to have the wedding of my dreams.

If that was not enough, Rebecca called me to tell me that she was leaving Prince because she found out he was cheating. She also said that there was no way that she could be in my wedding standing near or even in the same building as Prince. When I told Emmit about it, he told me not to worry. They had been through this several times over the years. He had no doubt that Rebecca would go to her parents' house for a week, then be back at her house with Prince the following week. I thought maybe I needed to find a backup just in case. This wedding planning became more painful than pleasurable.

I was thinking about an alternate for a bridesmaid when I received a call. Without looking at the caller ID, I answered, "Hello."

"Hey, ho," the unfamiliar voice said.

"Who is this?" I asked.

"Oh, you need a reminder? This is the one you called a bitch as you left my store and then you called my number one customer and told him that I was a criminal. Well, I did a little digging on my own and found out that you were marrying a doctor - the same doctor who is one of your favorite client's brother. Does the good doctor know?"

"Bitch, don't call me with this nonsense."

"Okay, I will call your fiancé."

"What do you want, Chardonnay?"

"I want $50,000 to keep quiet."

"What?"

"You heard me! Fifty stacks."

"I don't have that type of money."

"You are marrying a doctor, ho. You know how to turn a trick."

I could not believe this bitch who burnt down my club had the nerve to be talking to me like she was Porchia. Porchia was the only person that got a pass on that. "Why don't we meet to discuss this?" I asked.

"I want $50,000. There's nothing to discuss."

"Okay, let me get back at'cha," I said.

"Tomorrow."

"I will call you tomorrow," I responded and then ended the call.

I got off the phone and immediately called Prince to let him know what happened. Prince told me he had nothing to lose because his wife had left with the kids.

I reminded him that he had a brother to lose. He told me that everything would be taken care of and hung up the phone.

Later that night I was watching the evening news and saw that Chardonnay had been arrested on drugs and weapons possession. She evidently was rolling around with 100 kilos of cocaine and four semi-automatic assault weapons in her trunk. It looked as if Chardonnay would be gone for a little while this time.

Chapter 14

I was out meeting with the contractors about the house when Aunt Hattie called me frantic about some man being over at the house and about to tell Porchia that Duke was her daddy. I had come up with a story to tell Porchia why Pastor Charles had left money for her. I was going to tell her that Pastor Charles had a crush on her mom back in the day and how he just wanted to make sure she was taken care of because she looked so much like her mother.

Porchia was on her way to college and I did not want anything to interfere with that, especially not the DuBois Curse. If Porchia knew the man that she despised was her father, I don't know what she would do. Even more so, what would she do if she found out that I was her mother? I could not risk that. My heart dropped when Aunt Hattie said a man was there to tell Porchia about Duke.

"Aunt Hattie, what did you say?" I screamed.

"This man is here waiting to talk to Porchia about her insurance proceeds."

"Aunt Hattie, get rid of him anyway you can."

"How can I do that, Mystery?"

"Tell him that Porchia is out of town or something. I need time to figure something out."

"Okay, but I don't know when Porchia will be home. She went with Tracy to go get fitted for her dress."

"Get rid of that man now, Aunt Hattie!" I hung up the phone and told the contractors I would need to meet with them later.

The traffic leaving Sugarland was horrible. I turned on the radio and found out that there was a multi-car accident that would probably have the freeway traffic backed up for a while. I could hear a demon voice in my head saying, "I won! You could never win." started hollering in the car, "You will win over my dead body!" Then I started yelling at the cars to move.

I don't know how long I was stuck in traffic but I talked to myself and screamed the entire time. I prayed to God that Porchia would not arrive home before Aunt Hattie was able to get rid of the insurance man. I thought I had time because I thought that Porchia had to present the policy to the insurer and that they would not attempt to find her. I cussed at Duke for being part of the DuBois Curse.

The phone rang and interrupted my thoughts.

"Mystery, I had to tell her about Duke. She is in the bathroom going crazy."

"Aunt Hattie, I am on my way!"

I arrived and Porchia was locked up in the bathroom. I was so scared. I did not know what I was going to say. I heard Aunt Hattie's voice telling me,

"The truth shall set you free." My fear was that the truth would also set the DuBois Curse free. But at this point, I did not know what else I could do. If I told Porchia the half-truth and she found out the whole truth, she would hate me forever. And even more frightening, I don't know how she would react. Porchia was very hot-headed and could act irrational at times.

I knocked on the door, still not certain what I would say. Porchia told me to go away. I had to lie and say that Aunt Hattie had to use the bathroom. That is one thing that I knew: she would not do anything to hurt Aunt Hattie. Once I lured Porchia out of the bathroom, me and Aunt Hattie sat with her and told the story of her conception. I witnessed, for the first time, Porchia going ballistic on Aunt Hattie, and Aunt Hattie having no response to Porchia's rant. I realized that I was so obsessed with the DuBois Curse that I probably did not do the best thing by not telling Porchia the truth. But it was too late to have regrets.

I knew I would have to do everything in my power to help Porchia through this time. Porchia had been hit with so much over the last year that I was afraid this might take her over the top. Porchia let us know that she was disgusted with both of us, then retreated to her room. I gave Porchia a little time before going to check on her. She told me to leave her alone. Although I was concerned about her well-being, I thought it would be best to let Porchia calm down and attempt to speak with her in the morning.

I could not sleep, thinking about what Porchia was going through. She was on such a good course and headed for success. I drifted off to sleep for about two hours and when I awoke, I went to the bathroom to pull myself together to talk with Porchia. It was odd that Porchia had no clothes in the bathroom.

I knocked lightly on her door and there was no answer. I then said, "Porchia, can I come in?" There was no answer. I cracked the door open to see if she was still sleeping. She was not in bed. I opened it wide and she was not there. I then ran to the kitchen screaming, "Porchia! Porchia!" I went out to the backyard then immediately went to the front, but no Porchia. I ran into the house screaming, "Aunt Hattie! Porchia is gone!"

I immediately called Tracy to see if Porchia was with her. Tracy told me she had not spoken with her since yesterday. I called a couple of her teammates and none of them had seen her. I called Poo Man, Ty's cousin, and asked him if he had heard from Porchia. He said no but that he would check at the park to see if Porchia was there. In the meantime, I decided to go to the police station and report her missing. Prince was not on duty so I spoke to the officer in charge, who had so many questions that I did not want to answer.

"Well, Ms. DuBois, how long has your cousin been gone?"

I was not ready to announce that Porchia was my daughter so I told him my seventeen-year-old cousin was missing. "She went to her room last night. I woke up to talk with her this morning and she was gone," I answered.

"Has she disappeared before?"

"No, Officer. Never."

"Was there any argument or disagreement of any type?

I could not say that she found out her father was a child molester and her mama was a ho, as Porchia would put it, so I answered, "No, Officer. I am afraid that something has happened. I called all of her friends and no one has seen her."

"Is there any history of drug abuse, sexual abuse, or depression?"

"Officer, my cousin is a well-rounded honor roll student who would never run away. Something has happened and you need to search for her!"

"Ma'am, I am asking questions to determine where to start. Millions of teenagers run away from home. Sometimes you are unaware of problems. Where is her mother?"

"Officer, her mother died long ago. I can see that you won't help me so I guess I better organize a search party."

"I want to help you, but I need information to know where to start."

I got up and said, "Start with taking your head out of your ass."

I called Emmit to let him know that Porchia had disappeared. He asked me if I had checked with all of her friends. I realized that I had not checked with Ty.

I hung up with Emmit and immediately called Ty. Ty's phone went straight to voicemail. After about ten minutes, Prince called me and asked me what happened. I repeated the story to Prince and he said he would see what he could find out about Porchia's disappearance.

I went home and Aunt Hattie was pacing the floor. "Mystery, it is my fault. I will never forgive myself if something bad happens to Baby Girl."

I tried to comfort Aunt Hattie, but I was really worried myself. My mind started playing all sorts of tricks on me. I imagined Porchia being snatched up and being forced into prostitution. I then thought that maybe she was lying dead on the side of the road. Then I wondered if she had decided to run away and never come back again.

My whole life had been dedicated to making certain that the DuBois curse ended. Maybe I needed to pay more attention to my daughter. Just like my grandmother and mother, I failed at being a mother. Porchia was right; I was selfish and I thought about no one but myself. I would do anything to see her just roll her eyes at me one more time.

I searched for about three hours until I received an "Unknown Call."

"Yes," I answered quickly.

"Hi, Mystery. This is Ty. Porchia is in the hospital."

"What are you talking about, Ty?"

"She was hit by a truck near my house."

"Is she okay?"

"She is unconscious."

"Ty, why was she at your house?"

"I am not certain."

"What hospital?"

"The University of Alabama Hospital," answered Ty.

"Okay, Ty. I need to call the hospital right now."

"Mystery, I can send for you and Aunt Hattie and have a driver pick you up from the airport. I am going to be staying with Porchia at the hospital. Call me back when you are ready to come."

"Thanks, Ty. I am not certain Aunt Hattie should fly. But I will call you back when I am ready."

"Okay, I will be here."

"Ty, take care of my baby until I get there."

"I am not leaving her."

I ran to Aunt Hattie's room. She was just sitting there looking as if her best friend had died.

"Aunt Hattie, I found Porchia."

"Where is she? Is she okay?"

"No, she is not, Aunt Hattie. She went to see Ty and was hit by a truck."

Aunt Hattie screamed, "No! We gotta get there."

I did not have the heart to tell Aunt Hattie that she probably could not travel so I told her to pack some clothes. I called Emmit to tell him about Aunt Hattie but could not reach him. His answering service answered and said he was unavailable. I needed an answer right away whether Aunt Hattie could travel or not, so I said it was an emergency and asked to speak to a doctor that was on duty.

A doctor called me back within fifteen minutes and I explained the situation. He looked over Aunt Hattie's chart and told me that it would be fine for her to travel. He also told me to make certain that Aunt Hattie ate healthy and took her medication as she would if she were at home. I ensured him that she would.

I threw clothes together and Aunt Hattie and I were out of the house within the hour. I called Ty and he assured me that tickets would be waiting for us once we arrived at the airport. Not only were our tickets waiting, but he had bought us two first class tickets.

Aunt Hattie and I sat in silence for almost the entire ride, holding hands. I could see that Aunt Hattie was praying for most of the plane ride. I was not certain whether she was praying for Porchia or praying because she had never been on a plane. The weather was stormy and we had a bumpy ride most of the way. I could not have been happier when we landed at Birmingham airport.

Chapter 15

Shortly before we arrived at the hospital, the driver called Ty to come down so he could escort us to Porchia's room. Ty met us in the lobby. His eyes were red and puffy and looked as if he had not slept in days. He gave us each a hug and then escorted us to Porchia's room. Before we entered, I stopped Aunt Hattie and Ty and asked for us to pray. We all held hands and I was expecting Aunt Hattie to lead us in prayer, but to my surprise, Ty started praying.

"Dear Heavenly Father, I come to you with thanks in my heart for all that you do and continue to do for us. On this day, Lord, I am asking you to take care of Porchia. I know that You have all power in your hands, Lord. Please take your hands and deliver a complete recovery to Porchia. I ask for You to renew her heart, body, mind, soul and spirit. Lord, give us the strength we need to help Porchia through her recovery. Please let Porchia feel the love that we have for her so she can come back to us, Lord. We ask these things in Your son, Jesus's name. Amen."

When Ty finished praying, tears were flowing down Aunt Hattie's face. Aunt Hattie said, "That was a beautiful prayer baby."

Ty hugged Aunt Hattie and told her that it was in God's hand and that he believed that God would deliver Porchia back to us.

I looked at them and said, "I am ready to see Porchia now."

We walked in and I was not quite prepared for what I saw. My daughter was lying there looking lifeless with tubes running everywhere. Her face was black and blue and badly swollen. She was never a vain person and was not into how she looked, but she would be very upset if she saw herself right now. I grabbed Aunt Hattie and screamed, "My baby!"

"Mystery, we have to be strong for Porchia," said Aunt Hattie.

"Can she hear us?" I asked.

"The nurse say that we should talk to her as if she did hear us," said Ty.

"Ty, what happened?" I asked.

"I am not certain. I don't think she saw the truck when she walked into the street," said Ty.

"Why was she walking in the street?" I asked.

"Mystery, stop asking all of those questions. We need to stay prayerful and strong for Baby Girl," said Aunt Hattie.

"The doctor said he would be checking on her in about another hour or so. He will speak with you at that time about Porchia's medical condition," said Ty.

"Baby, do you need to go somewhere? Since we are here, you can do what you need to do," said Aunt Hattie.

"I don't want to leave just in case she wakes up," said Ty.

"We will call you if there is any change in her condition, Ty," I told him.

"Please, Mystery. Promise that you will call me if anything happens," said Ty.

"I will. You look bad. You probably would scare Porchia if she saw you like that," I said.

"Okay. I have a game tomorrow in town. I am supposed to be at practice, but I told my coach I just could not make it today. So I will be back once I clean up," said Ty.

"We will be here, baby," responded Aunt Hattie.

I noticed that the room was very nice. There was no other bed so I assumed that this had to be a private room. It had a big screen television, stereo system, and sofa sleeper with matching reclining chairs, mahogany dressers, a mahogany bookcase full of books, and a chair on the side of Porchia's bed. The windows opened up to a nice courtyard garden. I thought to myself, *Ty must have requested an upgraded room.* I told Aunt Hattie to sit in the chair next to Porchia's bed and I pulled over one of the recliners. Aunt Hattie was rubbing Porchia's cheek with the back of her hand, telling her that everything would be okay.

"Aunt Hattie, have you taken your medication?" I asked.

"I will in a little bit. I just need to be here with Baby Girl right now," answered Aunt Hattie.

I just sat there praying to God that Porchia would wake up.

The doctor came in about two hours later and said, "Hello, I am Jim Knight. I have been attending to Porchia since she was admitted."

I thought it was odd for a doctor to use just his first and last name. I stood up and said, "Hello, Dr. Knight. I am Porchia's mother, Mystery DuBois." It kind of sounded funny for me to say I was Porchia's mother. "And this is our aunt, Ms. Williams."

"Well, it is a pleasure to meet both of you," the doctor said.

"So Doctor, when will Porchia be waking up?" asked Aunt Hattie.

"Well, Ms. Williams, she has experienced trauma to her brain. This injury has caused Porchia to lose consciousness. We have been monitoring her and it seems that the swelling around her brain is decreasing and her brain activity seems to be increasing. The only thing we can do now is wait. And if you are a praying family, pray," said the doctor.

"Doctor, I keep Jesus on the main line," said Aunt Hattie.

The doctor smiled at Aunt Hattie and said, "Yes, and although His line might be busy right now, just hit redial."

"Yes indeed," said Aunt Hattie.

The doctor, while looking over Porchia and her charts, said, "I am off duty now, but I will be checking in on Porchia tomorrow."

"Thank you, Doctor. We will be here," I said. Once the doctor left, I looked at Aunt Hattie and softly said, "This is all my fault."

"No, baby, God has a plan. We don't question His plan but we know that all things work together for the good of those who believe in Him."

"I am not certain what type of plan includes my girl getting hit by a truck!"

Just as Aunt Hattie was about to start lecturing me about God and His plan, Ty walked in, looking fresh. He asked, "Was there any change in her condition while I was gone?"

"Well, the doctor just left. He said that looks like there is some improvement," I said.

"Have you two eaten? I can stay with Porchia while you go get something to eat," said Ty.

"That is a good idea. Aunt Hattie needs to take her medicine."

"I am right here, Mystery. I know what I need to do. But I really would like to stay with Porchia," said Aunt Hattie.

"We won't be gone long, I promise, Aunt Hattie," I responded.

"Aunt Hattie, would it be okay if I have some privacy with Porchia? There are some things I need to tell her."

"Sure, baby. I will go with Mystery to give you two a little privacy."

Ty kissed Aunt Hattie and said, "Thanks, Aunt Hattie."

I just shook my head. I was trying to make certain she remained alive and Ty just said he needed some privacy with Porchia, and she was willing to go.

Once we left Porchia's room, I realized that I had not spoken to Emmit. I turned on my phone and saw that he had left several frantic messages. I decided to get Aunt Hattie settled before returning his call. Aunt Hattie and I walked down to the hospital and before we could go through the line, Emmit called again. I ignored the call and Aunt Hattie and I went to get our food. After settling Aunt Hattie at a table with her food, I told her I needed to step away to make a phone call.

The phone rang before I could get to an open area. I answered it and it was Emmit. "Mystery, where the hell are you?"

I was surprised it was not "are you okay", but instead a question about where I was. "Hi Emmit, I am in Alabama. Porchia had an accident and she is unconscious."

"Did you ever think about calling me to let me know?"

"This is the first time I left Porchia's room. And my intent was to call you right away, but you called me before I could call you."

"That was very irresponsible of you, Mystery. I was worried about you. Don't ever let that happen again!"

Wow! I felt as if I was being scolded by a parent. "Emmit, I am sorry, but an emergency came up and all I could do is think about Porchia."

"I will be your husband and your first thought should be me," said Emmit.

I almost blurted to Emmit that no one would ever come before Porchia but I had not had the opportunity to speak with him about her. I thought that this was probably worth a face-to-face conversation.

"Emmit, I will speak with you later. I am trying to situate Aunt Hattie. She has not eaten or had her medications."

"Mystery, please call me back when you have time to talk."

I answered, "I will," knowing that I would call him back at my leisure. This was the first time I questioned whether Emmit was the right man for me. He did not even ask about Porchia's condition or about Aunt Hattie's well-being. They were my world and they needed to be part of his world too.

I found Aunt Hattie at the table looking very sad and just picking over her food. "What's the matter, Aunt Hattie, the food is not good?"

"No, baby. I am just worried about Baby Girl."

"Now Aunt Hattie, you always said that a person does not show faith when he worries about things that are in God's hand."

"I am scared, Mystery. I don't think I could love either one of you more if you were my own children. I raised Baby Girl, and it is not just right for her to be taken away from me right now. She has so much life ahead of her."

"You are right, Aunt Hattie, she does have so much ahead of her. She is not going anywhere yet."

Aunt Hattie looked at me and asked, "Do you think that young man has had enough time with her? I want to go back up."

"Sure. Just let me grab a salad to bring up to the room with me," I answered.

The truth was that I was also very worried, but I did not want to let Aunt Hattie know because of her delicate condition. Aunt Hattie and Porchia were all that I loved in this world. Without them, my world might as well end also. I didn't think God would be so cruel.

Chapter 16

Ty reserved us a room at a hotel near the hospital. However, we both stayed glued to Porchia's hospital room for three nights. On the fourth day, I was sitting talking to Porchia and her eyes fluttered. I thought it was my imagination. I decided to ask her whether she could hear me. When I asked that question, Porchia opened her eyes. I shouted to Aunt Hattie that she was waking up and she ran over to see her. We did a little celebration before Aunt Hattie told me to get the nurse.

Dr. Knight came into the room to examine Porchia. He told us that she was alert and astute. He also said that they would be running a MRI to ensure that everything was okay, but all her signs showed that she was on her way to an excellent recovery. He looked at all three of us and told us that although Porchia was awake, she still needed her rest and not to overdo it with conversation. I thought, *He does not know Porchia, because she is the one that will have a lot to say.* It was no surprise that she wanted to speak with Ty first. She started running the show as soon as she woke up. After

Ty, she had a conversations with Aunt Hattie. She saved me for last.

I was afraid that Porchia would pick up where she left off before running away, but she apologized to me for the way that she had treated me her entire life. None of that mattered to me. I was just happy that Porchia was back with me. She would never know how much I loved her, or that I would do anything for her. I just knew that I had to dedicate my life to making certain that she was happy.

I had been completely ignoring Emmit for the past few days. I spoke to him only once after the conversation where he reprimanded me for leaving without telling him. Our last conversation was very dry. I knew that I had some making up to do when I got home.

We left with Porchia three days after she woke up. Porchia was worried about school and making certain that she graduated on time.

Porchia got right back into the groove when we returned to Houston. I noticed that Porchia was a lot nicer, not only to me, but in general. She seemed to have more patience and she was a lot kinder. However, I wondered about what had happened between her and Ty. Ty left the hospital looking sad. He told us that he had several away games but that he would come to Houston to sneak in a visit with Porchia.

I was so glad that I was not working at the time so I could spend time with Porchia. Although we still did not have a mother-daughter connection, it was the first time I felt that we were connected.

I called Emmit to let him know that I was back in town. He told me that he needed to see me right away. I rolled up to the house and took out my keys as I normally did to get into the house. My keys were not working, so I rang the doorbell. Emmit came to the door in his robe.

"Babe, why are you still in your robe?"

"I was waiting for you." He took my hand and led me to the bed.

He made love to me passionately for about two hours. I had forgotten about his lovemaking skills when I was gone, but my memory returned after the first two minutes. No man had ever made me feel the way that Dr. Emmit Little did. I wondered if this was part of his medical training. He knew how to find every spot on my body and turn it into putty at his touch. I rolled over to give him a kiss and he stopped me and said, "Now you will know what you are missing."

"What are you talking about, babe?"

"Get dressed, get out, and never contact me again."

"What is wrong with you? I know that you are not mad because I had a family emergency and did not get your permission to leave town?"

"No. I don't want a spoiled woman."

"What are you talking about?"

"Porchia is your child. Not your cousin."

"Babe, I was going to tell you about that."

"When? When we were on our honeymoon trying to have our first child?"

"I don't know. The reason I did not tell you is because I have been trying to protect Porchia all of her life. She found out that I was her mother, and that is when everything went out of control. She ran away then ended up being hospitalized because she was hit by a truck."

"Mystery, please get up and get out."

"Are you serious?"

"Yes I am. My wife will be pure for me. I want my child to be her first child."

"Crazy-ass muthafuka! I was not pure when you met me."

"Yes, but I thought your womb was pure."

I did not know what to do. I was feeling so hurt but I could not let this man see me fall apart. I got up, grabbed my clothing, and left his house without looking at him or saying anything. I did not dress until I was outside of his house and I did not care who saw me. I sped away and the first place I saw where I could pull over, I stopped.

My mind started asking me all sort of questions. How could I have even thought about marrying a man like that? How could I have allowed him to have my mind, body, and heart? How could I have not known Dr. Little was psycho? I don't know how long I sat in my car and cried, but I knew I could not sit there forever so I pulled myself together to drive home.

Instead of driving home, I ended up at a bar. I started drinking Grey Goose Cosmos. I figured I could drown my problems in vodka and not feel the pain afterwards. After my fifth Cosmo, a man approached me and started a conversation.

I looked at him and said, "You may want to step away because I am ready to castrate a brutha right about now."

The man stepped away without any further conversation. I wanted one more Cosmo but knew that if I did not get home soon, Aunt Hattie would start worrying. I got up and stumbled toward the door. The bartender ran over to me and led me back to a seat. He told me that I was in no condition to drive and he called me a taxi.

I walked into the house crying only to see Porchia and Ty in the living room. I ran straight past them into my room. I must have scared Aunt Hattie to death, because she knows that I don't like shedding tears. I always thought tears were for the weak. Aunt Hattie started banging at my door and when I would not answer she busted in like the po-po's. I just fell into her arms and began crying even harder.

The next thing I knew, Porchia was in my room asking me what was wrong. I did not want Porchia to become involved in any of my nonsense. She had just come from a traumatic experience of her own. It was important that she lived her own life. I did not want her to start worrying about me and my broken life.

Porchia sat down next to me and insisted that I tell them what was wrong. I went into the story about how the doctor broke off our relationship because he did not want a woman that already had a child. I was surprised by Porchia's reaction. She was not only comforting and full of kind words, but she insisted that we all go out for a girls' night on the town. I went out with Aunt Hattie and Porchia and I partied like it was 1999. By the end of the night, I was asking, "Dr. Emmit Little who?"

The next morning I woke up with a hangover headache and a message from Dr. Little asking me to return the money that he had given me for the wedding budget and the engagement ring. He really must have thought I had just fallen off a turnip truck. Since there was not going to be a wedding, I thought I could leave my car at the bar I was at earlier because it was time to upgrade my ride. Thirty-five thousand dollars and whatever he paid for the ring would definitely assist me with that upgrade. I left a message for Dr. Emmit Little thanking him for the friendly reminder.

Chapter 17

After all of the madness, I woke up one day and decided to start planning the rest of my life. Porchia decided to take a scholarship to Georgetown University. I found Aunt Hattie another doctor and she lost weight and increased her physical activities. She was looking and feeling better than she had in years. I had been moping around and letting life pass me by because of what this man had done to me. I came up with the idea to open up a lunchtime entertainment venue. I wrote up my business plan and approached Big John with my idea.

Big John said, "Moneymaker, you have another great idea. The place will be a success just like what you have done in the past. I am not interested, but maybe Sweezy will like to get in on the action. He has been investing in a lot of different profitable businesses. I will hook you two up."

"Thanks, Big John. But I wish it was just you and me, because you let me do my thing."

"Only because it was you, Moneymaker. I don't trust too many people."

"Did I ever thank you for giving me a chance way back then?"

"Yes. Every week when the money rolled in."

Sweezy called me a few days after I spoke to Big John and asked to meet with me so he could hear my idea. Although I had everything completely figured out from the venue to the financing, I told him that I would get back in touch with him because I needed to complete the business plan. I remembered Sweezy as being the young, dumb, womanizing drug dealer that got Chanti killed for no good reason. Although he came highly recommended from Big John, I did not trust Sweezy and I would seek out other financing. I had a substantial savings but could not finance the club alone. Plus I liked having a little nest egg for unforeseen emergencies.

I went to different banks for financing, but it was evident after the fourth turn down that I would not get any financial institution to loan me the money. They all insisted that I did not have enough credit history for financing a business venture. I guess there is something to be said for paying things in cash instead of getting loans. After being rejected by the banks, I broke down and called Sweezy and we made arrangements to meet at This Is It for a lunch meeting.

I arrived and did not recognize Sweezy. He had lost 80 pounds and was looking more like Idris Elba than Biggie Smalls.

He reached out and hugged me and told me it was nice to see me. I gave Sweezy a half hug and a fake smile and told him it was nice to see him also. This Is It was packed with folks. Sweezy told me to wait a minute. He walked over and greeted a man with a brutha hug, and they both came back.

The guy said, "Please follow me." We were seated in a private area of the dining room.

"So how is Swoosh doing?" Sweezy asked while looking at the menu.

I knew that was Sweezy's nickname for Porchia.

"My daughter is doing great."

"Your daughter?"

"Yes. I figured you would hear soon enough."

"How did that happen? I guess I should not be surprised because you two look a lot alike. But you look like you can be sisters instead of mother and daughter."

"I was raped by Pastor Charles when I was a little girl."

"That sick bastard raped you too? We probably can blame every illegitimate child in the Ward on that man."

"Yeah, it was a long time ago. I just wanted to protect Porchia from all of that."

"I understand. You did what your felt was best."

"You are probably the only one who understands," I said.

"Yeah, and I wish Sister Carletta would have cut his dick off instead of killing him. That is too kind of a death for that bastard," Sweezy said. Without taking a breath, he asked, "So are you hungry?"

Sweezy waved over a waiter. He looked at me and asked if I was ready and I told him to go first. He ordered two entrees and a lot of different sides. I thought to myself, *He will pack back on all that weight eating like that.* Just listening to him order made me full, so I ordered the smallest entrée on the menu: turkey necks.

"So how do you plan on making us money?" asked Sweezy.

"Well, I want to open up a lunchtime gentleman's/woman's club."

"Aaah. So how would that work?"

"Well, it will cater to busy business professionals who may want to take a break during lunch for entertainment, dining, and relaxation," I said.

"So you think that you will have people spending their lunchtime there?" asked Sweezy.

"Yes. Besides the best meals in town, we will have live music, rooms with male and female strippers, pedicures given by men in G-strings, and massages performed by professional therapists."

"Well, that sounds good. But it sounds like a turned-up strip club to me," said Sweezy.

"No, Sweezy. The whole idea is to operate and manage a legal adult lunchtime entertainment venue."

"So you know what goes on at the strip club. You try to keep it legal and the girls wild out and do their own thang," said Sweezy.

"Our employees will be highly paid so we can discourage any type of prostitution happening at the site. They will have to sign an agreement that will state that our venue will have a zero tolerance policy for prostitution. This means that if any employee takes money for services rendered outside of the legal services we offer, they will be fired," I said.

"Girl, you turning me on right now, sounding like a lawyer. So how much will this venture cost me?" asked Sweezy.

"I already found the perfect spot for sale between downtown and the Medical Center. It is the right amount of space and all we need to do is go in and work on the inside."

"So how much?"

"Well now, I predict that we will clear about $100,000 a month after we get up and running."

"Are you going to share with me how much?" Sweezy asked again.

"About 1.5 million."

"Beautiful lady, you are too rich for my budget!" said Sweezy.

"Well, how much can you put up?"

"About half of that."

"Okay, I can get the other half. But I will be one-half owner of the club and paid a salary for operating and managing," I said.

"Why don't we operate and manage together so we both enjoy our profit?" responded Sweezy.

"What do you know about managing a club, Sweezy?"

"Nothing that I could not learn, since I have been part of several successful businesses and have gone to clubs most of my life," said Sweezy.

I did not like the idea of co-managing the club with Sweezy, but I was not certain who else I could go to for the money. I still was not sure where I would get the other half needed to get the club up and running.

Sweezy and I enjoyed our meal and spoke about what was happening in the hood.

I asked Sweezy about Jake. Sweezy told me that Jake was still serving time for burning down the club. According to Sweezy, Big John had forgiven Jake and would visit him often in prison. We both felt that Chardonnay was the devil in disguise and had taken down a good man. We departed after Sweezy had filled up on 10,000 calories by adding banana pudding to his already gluttonous meal.

****

I knew that I could make a club very successful, but I was concerned about getting the rest of the funding and co-managing the club with Sweezy. He seemed pleasant enough, but I did not know if he had the sophistication to operate this venue as I would like to see it run. I knew the first thing for me to do was to determine if I could get the additional funding.

I picked up the phone and called Big John and asked him if he could loan me $350,000. Without hesitation, Big John agreed and asked me when I needed the money. I told him that I would draw up a loan document with repayment terms included. After I hung up with Big John, I could see Aunt Hattie's Retreat coming into a life of its own.

Chapter 18

I was a little hesitant to use my money toward opening our venue, but I always knew that if there was no risk, there would be no gain. I realized that I was more excited about starting this business than I was about marrying Emmit. However, both planning the wedding and building the house kept me busy and content. Because of the house, I had made some good contacts with general contractors and construction workers, so I had the resources needed to turn the empty building into Aunt Hattie's Retreat.

I went to a former client who was a lawyer to write up a contract between me and Sweezy, as well as the repayment agreement to Big John. I never thought when I was working at The Club that I was building resources that could help me later on in life. Every former client that I contacted was always willing to help me with whatever I asked. As Aunt Hattie always proclaimed, "God is good all the time."

My relationship with Porchia improved as time passed. It still was not the daughter-mother relationship that I wished for, but it was far from the street fighter episodes we frequently had over the last seventeen years. However, since her accident, although she was much kinder toward me, something was different. She did not seem to be as happy as she was prior to the accident, though she had everything going for her. She was getting a full ride to the college that she chose, she had a rich boyfriend, and she had gained a sister that was already her best friend. Porchia spent as much time as she could with Tracy and her other brothers and sisters. I did not understand why she seemed so unhappy when she had her whole life in front of her.

One day I walked in and found Porchia in the living room with tears rolling from her eyes. "Porchia, what's wrong?" I asked.

"Nothing that I can't handle."

"Is everything okay with Ty?"

"Why would you ask that?"

I sat down next to her and said, "Well, I have not seen him around a lot these days."

"He does have a job, you know."

"I know, but I'm just trying to figure out what would have you in tears."

"Life, Mystery. I am going to be leaving my family, going to a new place, embarking on a new adventure. But I am actually comfortable with the life I have now."

"Porchia, it is called life. If you are lucky, you will go through different phases your entire life. That is called growth. If you live long enough, and I pray that you do, you will have both ups and downs. But life is not about the ups and downs; it is about how you deal with the ups and downs. And you must realize that you have a choice about how you deal with both the challenges and the successes."

"Yes, I know. I have had plenty of challenges over the last few months. I could have been broken but I had the strength to continue, thanks to the grace of God."

I nearly fell off the couch. I have never heard anything good about God coming from Porchia's mouth. I asked, "Did you say the grace of God?"

"Yes Mystery. I now know that He is an awesome God."

I hugged her and said what Aunt Hattie often said to me. "You will get through. Just hold on to God's unchanging hand."

We sat there and embraced for a while until Porchia said, "Okay, enough of the mushy stuff. So when are you taking me shopping? I need to be fly when I step off that plane in D.C."

"You don't need clothes to be fly. You are fly by genes alone," I said and laughed.

"Yes I am, but I still need to spend some of your money like I do so well," said Porchia.

"You do that all too well," I said, smiling. "How about this weekend?"

Porchia got up from the sofa, kissed my forehead, and said, "Thanks! You are the greatest."

That action caught me totally off guard, but it made me smile. I said, "I see. I just have to buy you off."

"You ain't got enough money to do that, Missy," responded Porchia as she left the room.

Although I was happy that Porchia was going to D.C., I was also sad. We were just starting a new relationship and I wanted a chance for it to develop. I knew that she would be busy with school and I would be busy with Aunt Hattie's Retreat. But I did not want Porchia to have any idea that I was also feeling sad. I definitely wanted her to step out and follow her dreams. She was the key to the DuBois Curse being broken.

I found Aunt Hattie out in the backyard with her garden. "Hey, Aunt Hattie."

"Well hello, baby. What have you been up to?"

"Just working on the business." I wanted to surprise Aunt Hattie that I was naming my business after her at the Grand Opening.

"So how close are you to opening?"

"Soon, Aunt Hattie. Very soon. And I expect you to be there."

"You could not keep me away, baby."

"Aunt Hattie, have you noticed something about Porchia?"

"Like what, baby?"

"I don't know. She is not as happy-go-lucky as she normally is."

"Baby, has she cussed you out lately?"

"No, Aunt Hattie."

"Has she tried to attack you physically?"

"No, Aunt Hattie."

"Well, has she called you a tramp?"

"No, Aunt Hattie, she has not."

"So what are you talking about?"

"I don't know. I guess it is just a mother's instinct. Something seems wrong."

"Baby, just enjoy your new relationship and everything will work out."

Aunt Hattie seemed like she knew something I did not know, but I thought I would let it go. "So Aunt Hattie, how are you feeling lately?"

"Baby, I feel like I am fifty again."

I laughed at that statement because fifty seemed pretty old to me. "Well Aunt Hattie, you are looking like you are forty."

"Girl, what you want from me giving me that compliment?"

"I just want to see you remain healthy and around for a long time."

"I will be around long enough to make certain that you and Baby Girl are okay."

"I need for you to walk me down on the aisle when I get married."

"Girl, you done found you another man?"

"No, Aunt Hattie. But I will never give up on love. My love right now is working on this business, but I will one day find the man for me."

"That's right. You know the Lord does answer prayers. Maybe not in your time, but He is always right on time."

"I am patient," I said.

"Patience is a virtue," said Aunt Hattie.

"Okay. I am going to cook something for dinner."

"Can we go out tonight?" asked Aunt Hattie.

I laughed. "What's wrong, Aunt Hattie? You don't like my cooking?"

Aunt Hattie chuckled. "No, it is not that, I just want to give you a rest."

"Okay. Let me see if Porchia wants to join us. How long will it take for you to get ready?"

"Baby, I stay ready. I am going to grab my shoes and purse," said Aunt Hattie.

When we arrived at the restaurant, Ms. Carletta and her entire family was there. Tracy asked us to join them. I was a little hesitant, but Tracy insisted. Aunt Hattie and I sat talking and laughing with Ms. Carletta and her parents. I could see a sparkle in Porchia's eyes as she talked with her younger sisters and brothers. At that moment, it seemed like we were all one big happy family. I imagined Duke burning in hell, watching his family at peace. That image brought a big smile to my face. Aunt Hattie looked at me as if she was reading my mind and smiled with me.

Chapter 19

When Porchia left to visit D.C., I missed her as soon as she walked through the security line, smiling and waving bye to me. My heart felt heavy and I felt as if I was all alone. Porchia had no idea how much I loved her and that everything that I did was for her.

I went to Aunt Hattie's Retreat to check on things and found Sweezy there with the contractors. He surprised me with how dedicated he was to our business venture and he was excited when I told him the name. He loved Aunt Hattie and thought it was a wonderful tribute to a beautiful woman.

Sweezy saw me and said, "Hey there, Queen. How are you doing today?"

"Not good. Porchia just left."

"Where did Swoosh go?"

"She went to D.C."

"But she is not done with school."

"She is just going for a visit to Georgetown."

"Swoosh is going to play ball at Georgetown?

"No, she is going to be some type of scientist."

"That's my girl. She has always been the smart one. Chanti would have been so proud of her. They were like sisters."

"Yeah, I know. I guess you still miss Chanti."

"I still feel guilty knowing that I was the intended target."

"You can't blame yourself. You did not pull the trigger."

"Well, there is a lot that I do blame myself for, but let's not have a pity party today," said Sweezy.

"Oh, sorry, Sweezy. I did not mean to bring you down."

"I would hate to see what you would do if you were trying to get a brutha down," Sweezy said, laughing.

"Okay. Come on. We have a lot to look forward to. Look at this place," I said while twirling around.

"You are funny. Let's go and celebrate with some caviar and champagne," said Sweezy.

"Where?"

"My place," said Sweezy. "I will drive."

Sweezy lived about twenty minutes from Aunt Hattie's Retreat in a suburb called Missouri City, Texas. We pulled into his neighborhood and my mouth dropped. All of the homes were at least 5000 square feet.

I looked at Sweezy and said, "Dang, Sweezy, I did not know you were living like this."

"You know I like to keep things low-key," answered Sweezy.

"You must be doing well with your other businesses."

"I am doing okay," answered Sweezy.

We pulled up to his house, which was surrounded by a big white iron gate. His house was a big white two-story plantation home with eight big white columns spread across the width of the home. The porch was decorated with two hanging swings and four oversized rocking chairs. I looked at Sweezy with disbelief. This man from the Ward who flaunted gaudy jewelry, women, and cars was now living like an elderly white couple on a plantation fairyland.

I walked into the house and the plantation theme continued. I felt like I was in Mississippi in the early 1800's. I looked at Sweezy and asked, "Why?"

"Why what, Queen?"

"What's up with your fascination with the plantation, brutha?"

"It reminds me of how far we have come."

"Why would you want to remember that?"

"Nothing wrong with remembering the past so you can successfully move forward. I guess that is your way of saying you don't like my house."

"It's not that. It's just surprising. I knew you lived in Missouri City, but I thought you would have a modern home."

"Hey, hold your opinions. You have not seen the kitchen yet."

Sweezy took me on a tour of his six bedroom, seven bath home. I thought the theater room was interesting, but what really shocked me was that he had a live-in Jamaican housekeeper and cook, Ms. Marvelle. She was a slim older lady with an infectious laugh and smile. Sweezy and I drank champagne and ate appetizers prepared by Ms. Marvelle.

Sweezy talked about his childhood. I found out that Sweezy grew up in different group homes. His mother died when he was young and he took to the streets at an early age. Big John took Sweezy in and raised him as his own. According to Sweezy, Big John was the reason why he was successful in all that he did. That day I found out that we had something in common besides the success of our business; we both had a fondness for Big John. And as bad as of our lives had been, we both had two people that cared for us who were not our blood relatives. Sweezy had Big John and I had Aunt Hattie.

We sat and talked about a variety of things unrelated to our gloomy childhoods or our blooming business. We started discussing TV shows and both of us were *Empire* fans so we went to his theater room and caught up on some episodes that we had missed. We talked and laughed like we were a couple of teenagers. After catching up on *Empire*, he talked me into playing Grand Theft Auto on his PlayStation 4. I beat him about three times and he was ready to switch to Call of Duty.

"You are a sore loser," I told him.

"And I never knew you were a cheater," he said, playfully putting me in a headlock.

"Stop it. You are messing up my hair."

"Queen, you don't have much hair to mess up."

I have worn my hair in a short bob-style-cut ever since I was fifteen years old.

"So? You are messing up what I do have," I said, laughing as he tickled me.

We looked up and Ms. Marvelle was standing with her hands on her hips. She asked whether we wanted to eat in her Jamaican accent. Embarrassed, I got up and straightened up my hair and clothes while Sweezy got up and said, "So what did you cook?"

"I made some curried goat, rice and peas, callaloo, plantains, and festival," answered Ms. Marvelle.

"Are you trying to show out for Mystery, Ms. Marvelle? I don't remember the last time you made me curry goat and festival."

"Just wanted to make certain your friend ate some good Jamaican food," said Ms. Marvelle.

"It is getting late. I probably should be getting home," I said.

"Girl, you gonna have Ms. Marvelle call up some of her distant cousins from Haiti and do some voodoo on you if you don't eat."

"Stop it, boy! You know I don't have no cousins in Haiti," said Ms. Marvelle.

"Shh, Ms. Marvelle. She don't know that."

"Okay, you two. I will stay."

Ms. Marvelle looked at me and smiled and said, "Thank you. I need some female energy in this house. That boy is just too much."

"Ahh, you know you could not live without me, Ms. Marvelle," said Sweezy.

I had never eaten anything other than jerk chicken. Ms. Marvelle's food was so good that I went back for a third helping. I was so stuffed when Ms. Marvelle came out with some brownies.

I looked and said, "I thought that the festival and the plantains were dessert."

Sweezy said, "Now Ms. Marvelle, you know that Mystery won't be able to handle your dessert."

"Speak for yourself," I said as I grabbed a brownie and munched it down.

It was one of the best brownies I had ever tasted. I asked for another one and Sweezy told me that I probably had enough.

"Don't tell me I can't have another one," I said as I started nibbling on another brownie.

Midway through the second brownie I started feeling lightheaded.

"Mystery, are you okay?" asked Sweezy.

"I don't know. I am feeling really good, but lightheaded."

"That is what I was trying to tell you, Queen. The brownie had some special medicine."

"What do you mean some special medicine?"

"It has marijuana."

"Oh no! You know I don't do any type of drugs, Sweezy."

"Marijuana is not drugs. It is a natural herb."

"If so, why am I feeling like this? I need to lay down."

Sweezy led me to one of his guest bedrooms. The last thing I remembered was Sweezy showing me the bathroom.

I woke up startled in a white tee. I went to the bathroom to freshen up. I heard Sweezy knocking on the door.

"Queen, are you okay?" he asked while walking in.

"Yeah, I am good. Did anything happen between us?"

"If something happened, you would definitely know."

"Don't flatter yourself, youngsta," I said, winking at Sweezy. "I want to take a bath. Where are your towels?"

"Yeah, I got your youngsta right here." Sweezy grabbed himself.

"Yeah, yeah. So where are your towels?"

"Look in the drawer next to the bathtub."

Sweezy had a big Jacuzzi bathtub that I could not wait to sit in and relax. I ran some hot water and found some foaming bubble bath, and bath salts to add to my water. He had a built-in Wi-Fi stereo system in the bathroom so I put on some light jazz. I relaxed in the bathtub, thinking about life in general.

I remembered that I had not spoken to Porchia and I decided I would call her after I finished my bath. After the thought of Porchia, I allowed myself to be carried away into tranquility. This was the first time in a very long time that I was able to relax without feeling the pressures from everything happening around me.

When I came out of the bathroom, Sweezy had laid a dress with tags on the bed and shoes on the floor in a box. It was a cute dress and shoes so I decided I would wear the outfit. At that time, Sweezy came into the room with my clothes washed and folded. He stopped dead in his tracks and stared at my naked body.

"Sorry, Queen. You look even more beautiful in your natural state."

"Where did you get these clothes?"

"I bought them for Chanti before she died."

"I can't wear a dead girl's clothes," I said, snatching my clothes from him.

"She never wore them or even saw them. I always shopped for her."

"I can't wear clothes that you bought for another woman."

"Okay, I hear ya."

I took my clothes and went into the bathroom to dress. When I came out, Sweezy was sitting on the bed.

He looked at me and said, "I hope I did not upset you. I have accepted Chanti's death and I am ready to move on. I don't know why I have not given away her clothes."

"I understand, Sweezy. It takes time." We embraced until my phone rang.

Chapter 20

By the time I made it home, Aunt Hattie was in her room. She was now used to me working late, so she did not worry much if I did not come home early. But I still thought that she did not go to sleep until she heard the door close. I was already relaxed but I thought a glass of wine would relax me even more. I went to the kitchen and before grabbing my glass, I saw a stack of mail, so I decided to look through it. I noticed that one card was some type of invitation.

It only had a return address and no name. I anxiously opened it and it was a wedding invite. It read, "Chardonnay Henry and Dr. Emmit Little graciously request your presence at their wedding…" I just stopped reading because I could not believe what I saw. This bitch would not stop until she attempted to take everything I ever had. I decided to pour my glass of wine and retire to my room without giving them a second thought. I thought about calling Porchia, but realized she was an hour ahead of us and probably fast asleep.

I went to bed calm but woke up mad as hell. What was Emmit thinking, marrying a ho turned criminal? I called Prince to get the scoop. He told me that there was a problem with overcrowding, so Chardonnay received an early release from prison. According to Prince, Emmit met Chardonnay at a hospital charity event for kids. She approached him and they had been inseparable ever since that night. Prince told me that Chardonnay moved into Emmit's place after two weeks of dating, and Emmit proposed to Chardonnay two weeks later. I asked Prince what he was going to do about it and he said nothing, because Chardonnay had Emmit's nose wide open.

I called Sweezy to tell him about what happened. He talked me into standing down. He said, "You don't have to do a dayum thang, 'cause karma is a bitch." He went on to tell me that the mother of the guy who killed Chanti was killed by a drive-by shooter two weeks after he had killed Chanti. I listened to Sweezy and thought that maybe Emmit and Chardonnay deserved each other.

I called Porchia after hanging up with Sweezy. She sounded happy and busy.

"Hey, Mystery, is everything okay?"

"Yes. I am just checking on you."

"Just been real busy. Hey, can't talk right now, but I will call you back later."

"Okay, do that. Love you."

"Love you too! Give Aunt Hattie a kiss for me!"

"Okay, talk with you soon." I said.

I was so glad that she was getting away from Houston. She would have a chance of making something out of her life without all of the drama that the Ward brings. Porchia was well-grounded and she could probably rise above any circumstance, but it seemed like people here did things with the intention of holding you down.

I could not stop wondering why Chardonnay had it in for me. I never had any previous contact with her prior to her working at The Club. I thought me knocking her unconscious was water under the bridge. Evidently, she still had beef. I was going to have to figure out a way to get her out of my life forever.

I was thinking about what I could do to make it happen when the general contractor called to tell me that we were having a difficult time getting the city to clear the electrical work. Every time the inspector came out, he would find another problem. I told the contractor to call Sweezy and ask him to take care of it. I was not feeling well, and frankly I was tired of having to solve every problem that came up. Since we were partners, I figured it was time for him to become involved in troubleshooting. As it turned out, Sweezy knew someone at the inspector's office and was able to quickly resolve the problem.

I lounged around in my sweats all day until Aunt Hattie approached me and said, "Baby, what is going on with you? I never see you pouting around the house all day."

I really did not want to get into this issue about Chardonnay with Aunt Hattie. I was still trying to figure out how I could get her out of my life. I told

Aunt Hattie that I was not feeling well. She asked me what was wrong and I told her I just felt yucky.

"I got something for yucky," Aunt Hattie said as she left me and went to whip up one of her concoctions in the kitchen.

I usually speak to Aunt Hattie about everything, but this situation seemed petty. But although it was petty, it was driving me crazy. I was not necessarily upset at Emmit, but I wondered how far Chardonnay would go in attempt to hurt me before she stopped.

I remembered Aunt Hattie telling me a little while back that someone had called Porchia and told her that she and Tracy had more in common than she thought. This was before Porchia knew that I was her mother or that Duke was her father. It made me wonder whether that was Chardonnay attempting to hurt Porchia. I then realized that I would definitely have to do something because if she hurt Porchia or Aunt Hattie in any way, I would go to jail for murder.

Aunt Hattie walked into the room with her concoction and told me to drink it. I pretended to sip it and she said while walking back into the kitchen, "You should be feeling well in no time."

I was not sure what I would have to do to Chardonnay. I put her in the hospital and jail and the bitch still was coming after me. I called one of my former clients, Joe, who was rumored to put people away permanently. I could not take the chance that Chardonnay would do something to hurt Porchia after she realized that she could not hurt me. And although

I did not want Chardonnay put away permanently, I would like her in a position that she could not get around easily to cause any additional pain to me or my family. I met with Joe and told him what I needed. He said he could arrange for that to happen, but it would cost me. We negotiated a price of $25,000 to get the job done quickly.

The next day I drove to meet Joe at a gas station across town. I pulled into the agreed meeting spot and nervously waited for him to come. I thought about backing out, but knew that if I did not protect us, we would get no protection from Chardonnay. I was deep in thought when I heard a knock on the window. I looked up and it was Prince.

I rolled down the window and asked, "Prince, what are you doing here?"

"Trying to save your life."

"What do you mean?" I asked.

"You don't want to spend a lifetime in prison over some bullshit."

"Prince, what are you talking about?" I asked.

"Stop trying to play me, Mystery. Joe is a police informant and you are lucky he came to me. You know that I am fond of you and would never let anything happen to you."

"Oh my God! That snitch!"

"You should be thanking God because all of this could have gone down very differently."

"Prince, I was just trying to stop that bitch before she does something crazy to me or my family."

"Look, Mystery, leave that to me. I am keeping a close eye on her. You know the saying, 'Keep your enemies close and your friends even closer'? Well, she will be a relative and my eye will be all over her. As a matter of fact, I am befriending her to make sure she stays in line. I don't trust an arsonist around my family."

I began violently shaking. I could not believe that I was going to this extent to get rid of Chardonnay. I could have gone to prison and would forever be away from Porchia and Aunt Hattie. I told Prince that I was sorry and glad that he came to save me. He responded that he was glad that he was there to save me too. He saw that I was upset and asked me if I needed him to drive me home. I assured him that I was okay and he told me that he would call me later.

I sat in that spot for hours, wondering what the hell was wrong with me. I would have never thought of hurting an animal much less a person. If I did drugs, this would have been a time I would have indulged just to numb my feelings. My mind was racing and my heart was trying to keep up. I picked up the phone and called Sweezy.

"What's up, Queen?" asked Sweezy.

"I almost did something crazy."

"Want to talk about it?" asked Sweezy

"No. Not really."

"Why don't you come over?"

"I don't think I can drive."

"Where are you? I will come to you."

I was startled when Sweezy knocked on my passenger window. I opened the door and he got in.

"Mystery, you don't look good at all. Do you need to go to the hospital?"

"No, I feel okay physically, but I am not doing good mentally. My brain is moving entirely too fast."

He got out of the car and came to my side. He then took my keys and purse, locked my door, and led me to his car, where he put me on the passenger side. He made a couple of calls and the next thing I knew we were at the airport and boarding an airplane.

"Where are we going, Sweezy?"

"Just relax and leave it all up to me."

He gave me a pill and some water. I did not even fight or bother to ask him what he was giving me. I took the pill. I woke up when I heard a flight attendant announcing that we were arriving. I still did not know where we were, but when I looked down I saw beautiful clear blue water. I looked at Sweezy and he was smiling.

"Where are we, Sweezy?"

"We are landing in Puerto Vallarta."

"I can't be in Puerto Vallarta. I have Aunt Hattie to take care of! And not to mention Aunt Hattie's Retreat. What about my BMW in the parking lot?"

"Don't worry, Queen, I got this. All I need for you to do is relax."

"Okay, but Porchia will be coming home from D.C."

"You will be back before Porchia gets back."

I was so used to controlling my environment and circumstances that I did not feel comfortable letting someone handle things unless I gave them permission to do so and specific instructions. I was about to argue with him when he put his finger on my lips and said, "Queen, please let me take care of you for the next few days."

I felt at that point, I could not do or say anything but accept his request.

Chapter 21

I spent the next two days in bliss. Sweezy owned a house on the beach. During the mornings we would walk to the market and get fresh fruit and seafood. During the evenings we walked the beach and watched the sun go down. At night we found non-tourist restaurants where we could eat, drink margaritas, and take shots of tequila. The best part of it was that not once did Sweezy attempt to have sex with me.

We talked, laughed, and enjoyed each other's company. I probably shared more information about myself with Sweezy than I had ever shared with any other living individual, including Aunt Hattie. We discussed fears, dreams, failures, successes, hopes, and desires. I even told Sweezy how I viewed him before we entered our business arrangement. Meanwhile, Sweezy revealed to me that he had always had a crush on me and one day hoped that we would be friends. I told him that day was definitely here. He gave me a friendly hug and kiss on the cheek.

I was not ready to leave when the time came. I felt no stress and more free than I had ever felt. Although I had arrived with only the clothes on my back, by the time we were ready to leave, I had three suitcases full of clothes, shoes, liquor, and souvenirs. Sweezy threatened to leave me in Puerto Vallarta if I bought one more thing. I usually did not spend a lot of money on myself because I was so busy saving for Porchia's college fund. It felt good to go shopping, not only for myself, but also for Porchia and Aunt Hattie.

We arrived home and everything was on track. The contractors were successful at getting their inspections and Aunt Hattie's Retreat was about two months from completion.

Ms. Carletta had spent time with Aunt Hattie during my absence. Aunt Hattie could not stop talking about the good time they had catching up and talking about old times. I spoke to Porchia while she was in D.C., and she had nothing but good things to say about her experience there. She loved her professor, she knew her roommate through Ty, and she had met an Indian boy that she could not stop talking about.

I was excited about picking up Porchia from the airport, but she told me that she had a ride. I don't know what happened in D.C., but the day she came home she was a different person than when she left. I walked in on her and Aunt Hattie dancing around the kitchen table. She grabbed me and just hugged me and Aunt Hattie and told us that she loved both of us. She did not have to say one word because I felt her love. If

I could have held on to the feeling I felt at that moment for the rest of my life, my life would have definitely been one worth living. But as my saying goes, all good things come to an end.

A few weeks later, I woke up one morning and Aunt Hattie was not yet up. I figured she was tired, so I decided to let her sleep in. After I thought she had probably slept long enough, I walked into her room to wake her up. The minute I walked into the room I knew something was wrong. I always felt Aunt Hattie's spirit, but on this day I felt only a cold stiffness in the air. I called out to Aunt Hattie and she did not answer. I went to the bed and shook her and she did not move. I started yelling and she did not move. I realized that something was wrong and called the paramedics.

I sat with Aunt Hattie, holding her hand, pleading with her to come back. The paramedics arrived, took vitals, and rushed her out of the house. However, I knew in my heart that Aunt Hattie was gone. I rushed to the hospital only to find out what I already knew. Aunt Hattie had died.

I broke down at the hospital. This was surprising because I could count the number of times I had cried in my life on one hand. The most recent was when Emmit broke off our engagement in such a cruel manner. Aunt Hattie would always tell me it was okay to cry. But I always viewed crying as a sign of weakness.

I gave myself permission to cry because I felt weak. I had lost my foundation, my guide, and my rock. Then I thought about Porchia. I don't know how I was going to share this information with Porchia. I knew that Porchia trusted and loved Aunt Hattie more than any other person in the world. I did not know how Porchia would deal with Aunt Hattie's death. I knew that she was trying hard to like me, but I could never be to her what Aunt Hattie was to her. I think that hurt me more than knowing that Aunt Hattie was gone.

When I pulled myself together, I called Mr. Ashton, who was both the principal at Porchia's school and one of Aunt Hattie's best friends. He took the news very hard. I told him I would be there to pick up Porchia. He told me that I should not be driving and he would drive Porchia home. I wanted to pull myself together to be strong for Porchia. The minute I saw her face, I broke out in tears again. I didn't know how either of us was going to make it now. Aunt Hattie was strong enough for both of us, and I knew with her by our sides, we could do anything - even beat the DuBois Curse.

I began suffocating because of the number of people around, so I decided to escape to the kitchen with Ms. Carletta. When I walked into the kitchen, she was preparing to cook.

"Ms. Carletta, what are you doing?"

"When I get nervous, I cook."

"You don't have to cook."

"No, I don't, but I want to cook. Are you okay?"

"No, I am not," I answered.

"Mystery, I know you have been through a lot, but remember, you are never alone."

"I know. I have Porchia."

"Yes, you have Porchia, but you also have God."

"Aunt Hattie always told me that. But sometimes I feel as if He does not know that I exist."

"You have been through a lot, but He is has been here for you. Everyone around you has been praying for you, including me. I know what my husband did to you and that is unfair for anyone to have to deal with, especially a child."

"I just think that people use excuses not to succeed. Excuses don't work for me. I have to succeed regardless of my situation or circumstances."

"Yes, God provided Aunt Hattie to you as your role model. You have inherited a lot of her traits. You are a fighter, you are determined, and you are strong. But there is one important trait that she had that you have yet to show."

At that point I wanted to tell her to mind her own business, but I thought I would let her talk. "So what is that?" I asked.

"Her faith. She had more faith than I have ever seen from a person. You probably don't know this, but after what my husband did to Tracy, you, and all of those other young girls, I blamed myself. When I was released from jail, I could not face my children, my parents, or anyone else. I was just ready to die because I felt so guilty."

"That is all good, but how did Aunt Hattie's faith help you?" I asked.

"Hattie told me that I had to believe that God would be there to get me through. She read Scriptures to me and called me every day until she felt I had the strength to carry on. But she had enough faith for the both of us. That is when I realized that if I trusted in God the way she did, I would be able to live again. I am so glad that I did! I have never been happier or had a stronger relationship with God. I give all glory to God for putting Hattie Mae Williams in my life. And you can have that same joy that I wake up with every day, regardless of what is going on around you."

I could not speak or ask any more questions. I had tears rolling from my eyes as I thought about Aunt Hattie and her strength, her wisdom, and her faith. I owed it to her to be the woman that she knew that I could be.

Ms. Carletta came and put her arms around me and said, "Don't worry. You will make it through."

Someone walked through the door and cleared his throat and I looked up and it was Sweezy.

He said, "I am sorry, am I disturbing you?"

"No, baby, come right on in," said Ms. Carletta.

Sweezy walked toward me and said, "I just wanted to come and check on you and Swoosh. I am so sorry, Mystery."

I looked at Ms. Carletta and asked, "Will you be okay? I need to speak with Sweezy."

"Go on, baby, I am fine. You know I have the Lord as my comforter."

"Thank you, Ms. Carletta," I said as I went out to the backyard with Sweezy.

We sat on the bench that Aunt Hattie had set up in the backyard among her flowers. Sweezy looked at me and said, "I could not believe it when I heard the news."

"I never expected this, Sweezy. She was looking so good, and I thought she was doing well."

"I know. Life has so many unexpected twists and turns. Sometimes I get dizzy."

I laughed at his description and said, "You have a way with words."

"I know. I have been through a lot the last year and a half."

"Sweezy, do you believe in God?"

"Queen, I fell on my knees and submitted myself to Him after Chanti's death. I would not have gotten through that time without believing and trusting in Him."

"I thought I believed in Him too until I realized I put more faith in Aunt Hattie than I did in God. I wonder if that is why He took her away from me."

"God has a plan so great that you could never imagine it. Just know that He has the master plan," said Sweezy.

"Would you pray with me right now?" I asked.

"Sure," Sweezy said as he grabbed my hand. "Would you like for me to lead the prayer?" he asked.

"No. I need to speak with Him," I responded.

"Dear Heavenly Father, I have come before you many

of times in prayer but never in complete submission and belief in your power. Lord, I ask for you to forgive my ignorance and accept my submission to your will. As you know, Lord, Aunt Hattie has been my guiding light, but I am now looking toward you for direction, advice, and comfort. Lord, I now have to lead this household and be a guide for Porchia. Please provide me with the wisdom and strength I will need to carry on in your name. Lord, I thank you for placing people in my life that will help me through this time. Lord, I thank you for Sweezy being here at this moment. May you continue to look over him and provide for his needs. I am asking all of these things in your Son Jesus's name. Amen.

"Amen! That was a righteous prayer, Mystery."

"Hopefully it will be a start to a growing relationship," I said.

It startled me when Sweezy leaned over and kissed me, and I kissed him back.

Pulling away after a while, I asked, "Where did that come from?"

"I don't know. I just felt it was right at the moment. Did you not like it?"

"Yes, I did." I then bent over to kiss him.

Chapter 22

The next few weeks I saw a very different side to Porchia. It started with her asking me if I minded if she made the arrangements for Aunt Hattie's funeral. I was not looking forward to picking out a casket, determining the order of service, or any of the stuff that went along with losing a loved one, so I happily agreed. She made all of the arrangements while I worked on opening Aunt Hattie's Retreat, which meant even more to me now than when I first started.

Porchia gave Aunt Hattie a royal home-going service that looked like it took place in a flower shop. There were so many beautiful flower arrangements in purple and white alongside Aunt Hattie's purple casket. Aunt Hattie would have looked like she was sleeping with her Bible in her hand, with the exception of the St. John's suit that Porchia had purchased to lay her to rest. She looked like a defense attorney that was praying about winning her high profile murder case before entering the courtroom.

Porchia seemed to have the world in the palm of her hands. She was graduating with high honors and also making preparations to attend Georgetown. She and Ty seemed to be on track and he had visited her several times. She also developed a relationship with Ms. Carletta's family and she would spend a lot of time at their home.

Aunt Hattie's Retreat was going to be opening in a few weeks. Sweezy and I spent a lot of time together, both doing business and having fun. I grew very fond of Ms. Marvelle and her cooking. I must have put on at least five pounds hanging out at Sweezy's house.

One night after a great meal and drinking red wine, Sweezy said he wanted to talk about us. I asked him, "What about us?"

"I want more for us," said Sweezy.

"What do you mean more?" I asked.

"I want for us to be a couple."

"But Sweezy, you are my best friend."

"Yes, Queen. That is what makes it great."

"What do you mean?"

"Don't you want your mate to be your best friend?" Sweezy asked.

"Well, I never thought about it like that," I said.

"You know about the homie, lover, friend, don't you?"

"That sounds like something a child molester might say," I said, laughing.

"Look. We enjoy each other's company. We like the same things. We make each other laugh," he said.

"Yeah, but we have a seven year age difference between us. When I am in my mid-thirties, you will still be in your twenties. And don't say age ain't nothing but a number," I said.

He leaned over to kiss me and said, "I am not going to tell you. I will just show you."

I enjoyed his kiss but I looked at him and said, "Yeah, but a kiss does not mean that we will make it as a couple."

"You are right. It is everything else I said. We are compatible all the way around."

"I just don't want to mess up our relationship, Sweezy."

"I don't either. I just want to make it permanent. Just give us a chance."

I picked up my glass to toast and asked him to pick his glass up too. We clicked our glasses together and I said, "To chances."

Sweezy added, "And everlasting love."

I thought, *What the hell?* I had not been successful with past relationships. Why not try to see what happens with my friend and business partner?

****

We had a successful opening. Everyone who was everyone came to our "Open House" where we had a variety of entertainment. I wanted Porchia to be a part of our opening, but since she was not yet eighteen, she could not attend. However, she helped me pick out my dress, shoes, and accessories for the night's festivities.

I really thought that she could be a fashion designer because she had a great eye for fashion. She also could have been a model because she was tall, thin, and beautiful. I teased her because she had a little bump on her back. Although thin, she had a great shape with a little booty. I was probably the same size with the exception of having much more booty and breasts.

After everyone left, Sweezy asked for us to christen the place. I told him that it was too late to have someone come and pray over the place. We should have done it prior to opening. He laughed at me and took me onto the stage and began kissing me. He then went down to my neck, nibbling and lightly sucking on it. Although we had agreed to try a relationship, we had never done anything more than kiss. He then went down my dress and starting nibbling on my breasts through my sweater. I started getting really hot.

He stopped and led me over to the piano and put me on top of it. He slowly pulled off my shoes and began kissing my feet. He then worked his tongue and lips up my legs. When he got to my knees, he looked up and said, "My, my, Queen, what big knees you have."

I playfully slapped him on his bald head and told him to shut up and continue what he was doing.

He continued his teasing and worked his way up to my thighs. He spread my legs and played around my inner thighs with his tongue. I thought I would explode. He then worked his way to my panties and began teasing my clit through my soaked panties.

He looked up and said, "Looks like someone is excited."

I was panting so much I could not respond.

We worked our way through every room in the club, and two hours later, I was beyond satisfied. Sweezy was smiling from ear to ear as we both got into our cars and went our separate ways.

Sweezy asked me to attend an airshow with him at Ellington Field. I had never attended an airshow, but I had seen the Blue Angels on TV and thought that it would be exciting to see in person. I was excited about going, but Sweezy was overly-excited about going. He rushed me out of the house and said we had to arrive for the first show. When we parked, he rushed me up to the place where they had the stands. We got situated and he said, "Oh good, they have not started!" He reminded me of a kid waiting for Santa to bring presents on Christmas Day.

The show started twenty minutes late. I was impressed with what I saw, but it was nothing that I would have to rush to go and watch again. The Flying Eagles were almost done with the show when they started swooping around in the air. When they finished they had written, "Will You Marry Me Mystery?" I looked over at Sweezy and he had that goofy smile he wears when he has done something special.

I screamed, "You are crazy! But yes!" We began kissing and the people around us burst out with cheers and applause.

We rode home talking and laughing. I then thought of Porchia and how I would break the news that I was getting married. Then I thought about Chanti and how Porchia would take the news about me marrying

Chanti's love. I became quiet and Sweezy asked me what was on my mind. I told him that I was concerned about breaking the news to Porchia.

He said, "Porchia is a well-grounded young woman and I am certain that she would want to see us both happy."

I was not as confident about that as he was. I asked him not to say anything to anyone about our engagement until I had a chance to speak with Porchia.

He agreed and said, "Queen, no one will believe you because you have absolutely nothing to show for it. Writing in the sky does not count."

"Oh, that is what you think. I snuck in a picture. But you better be saving your pennies for a big-azz ring for my pretty little finger."

"No doubt. I have been looking at some big zirconias," he said, smiling.

"You know what you can do with your zirconia! I am trying to practice a more Christ-like behavior, so I will let you use your imagination."

"In case you did not know, your thoughts count too," Sweezy said.

I walked into the house, ready to share my news with Porchia, but when I walked in, Chardonnay was sitting in the living room talking with Porchia. I said to myself, *God, are you testing me?*

Porchia looked up at me and said, "Hey, Mystery. Your friend stopped by and we were just choppin' it up."

I looked at Porchia and said, "Do you mind leaving us? We have a lot to catch up on."

"It was nice meeting you Chardonnay. Hopefully I will see you soon."

"The same to you, Porchia, and congratulations on your scholarship. I would love to get that invite to your graduation."

"Sure thing. I will get your address from Mystery."

"Mystery, you certainly have a smart daughter."

"Why are you here?"

"I am here to call a truce."

"I did not realize that there was a battle," I calmly responded.

"For your information, I did not marry that jerk. He did not want me, he wanted you. He wanted me to talk like you, laugh like you, and dress like you. I drew the line when he wanted me to cut my hair just like yours," said Chardonnay.

"I don't care who you marry or don't marry. You need to leave my house now or I will call the police."

"I am not here to give you any problems. I want to talk with you."

"We have nothing to talk about, Chardonnay."

"Yes, we do. Please hear me out."

"You have nothing that I want to hear."

"I beg to differ with you."

"Look, if you don't get - "

Before I could finish my sentence, she blurted out, "I am your sister."

I wondered what the hell this girl was up to now? "What are you talking about?"

"Our grandmother made our mom give me away when I was born."

"We don't have the same mother!"

"Yes, we do. The mother who raised me told me the story on her death bed."

"Chardonnay, I am not certain why you are here making up this story, but I am not interested."

"That is the reason I did those bad things to you. Our mom gave me away, but she kept you when you were born. You had the opportunities that I never had. My adopted mom was a drunk. I don't recall one day when she was sober. She even took me to kindergarten drunk. But you grew up with a woman who loved you, and put you and your child first in everything she did."

"You don't know the trauma I encountered as part of my childhood. There is nothing to be jealous about."

"But you got everything handed to you. I worked hard for everything and still could not get anything. I am nothing."

"That is not my problem, Chardonnay. I think you are sick to make up that story."

"I knew you would not believe me, so I brought you this contract."

She handed me a piece of paper. I looked at it and it was an agreement between my grandmother, Eva, and some lady named Anne that she could have my mother's child, Chardonnay, in exchange for $5000 and for not revealing her real birth mother. The paper was signed by my grandmother Eva, Prosperity, and Anne.

"This does not prove anything. It is a piece of paper with writing. Anybody could have written it and signed it."

"My mom was trying to get pregnant but she miscarried several times. Her husband thought it was her fault so he told her that he was leaving her. She wanted to keep her husband, so she faked a pregnancy, then bought a child, which was me."

"You said you had a drunk mom, but what happened to your dad?"

"Her husband found out that she had bought a baby when I was six months old. I don't have any memories of him because he left her and never returned."

"Chardonnay, you may need mental help."

"Mystery, please take a DNA test. You will find out that we are related."

"I don't care about that. You have done so much to ruin any chance of a relationship, even if we are related."

"I am so sorry, Mystery. I hope you find it in your heart to forgive me. I have no other family but you and Porchia. I just hoped that we could be family."

"I am sorry too, Chardonnay, but I am going to have to ask you to leave."

Chardonnay grabbed her bag and said, "I will just keep on praying for us."

I did not know what to believe after Chardonnay left. Could there be some truth to her story? The only ones who knew the truth were dead. I knew that somehow, I would have to find out if Chardonnay was telling the truth. Until then, I would not share this with anyone - not even Sweezy.

Chapter 23

We were busy with Aunt Hattie's Retreat. It became a sensation around Houston and the surrounding area. Businesses were contacting us and reserving private corporate retreats. It was amazing the prices people were willing to pay to rent out our club. I thought it would take at least a year to recoup the money that we put into the club, but within three months, we were in the positive.

I called Big John and asked him to meet me for lunch at Joe's Crab Shack. The first thing he said when he saw me was, "Congratulations."

Despite me asking Sweezy to keep our engagement quiet, he told me that he had to let Big John know. I asked Sweezy not to let another person on this earth know. He assured me that he did not have any other person on this earth to tell.

Big John asked me how things were going. I gave him the update and handed him a check for $400,000.

Big John asked, "What is this?"

"That is payment for the loan you gave me," I responded.

"I loaned you $350,000, not $400,000."

"The rest is interest. I really appreciate it."

He handed me the check back and said, "No, I appreciate you and everything that you have done for me. This is your wedding present. Just promise me you will take care of my boy."

"Big John, I can't accept this."

"Not only can you, but you will. You don't want to get on my bad side."

I got up from the table and gave him a big, wet, mushy kiss on his cheeks.

"Girl, stop all that. You know how people talk in H-Town."

Big John and I grubbed on some crabs. After we killed the crabs, we said our goodbyes. I never thought about it before, but Big John was like the daddy I never had. He always watched out for me. Now he would be able to see his two children marry. He was such a good man. I wondered why he did not have any children of his own. Ever since Cherelle died, he never got serious about another woman. I took a mental note to help Big John find a good woman.

I was driving to Aunt Hattie's Retreat when I got a call from Sweezy. "Hey Queen, some man came by the club to see you."

"Who was he?"

"I don't know, but he said he had some personal business to speak with you about."

"What was his name?"

"He left his business card for you. Let me see. His name is James Henry. Queen, you know you are not supposed to trust a man with two first names?"

"I should not trust a man named 'Sweezy' either," I said, laughing.

"Yeah, and I should not trust a woman with a big butt and a smile either. But I trust you."

"Alright now. Those are fighting words, youngsta. Are you at the club?

"No, I am out shopping for spa items."

"Okay. Can you text me the number?"

"I will. You know I love you, right?"

"I love you too."

I was anxious to find out about this mystery man who visited the club and told my fiancé that he had some personal business with me. I called the number and there was no answer, so I left a message with my number.

Although I was preoccupied by things going on around me, Chardonnay had me twisted. I contacted Prince to get his lead on a private investigator. I met Detective Wright at his office near the Galleria. I walked in wearing a big floppy hat, sunglasses, and a dark suit, looking like a damsel in distress from a movies in the forties. Detective Wright was a retired police officer from HPD. He was a small Black man that looked like he was constipated. He had a lisp when he spoke, so it took me a while to understand all of his questions. He asked for $5000 upfront, but he said that he thought that it would cover the price of finding out if Chardonnay was telling the truth.

When I was leaving, I asked, "So Detective Wright, how long will it take?"

He responded, "I'm fath. So I would say a couple of weekth."

At least I sort of understood what he was saying that time.

I shook his hand and he said, "It was a plather to meet you Mytree."

I had strained so much to try to understand what he was saying that by the time I left his office I had a headache and I was confused about what I was supposed to be doing next. I thought to myself that Prince should have warned me about the lisp so I would have been prepared. As I was driving off, my phone rang but I did not recognize the number. Perhaps it was Detective Wright with another question. I really did not feel like going through that again. I answered the phone and it was James Henry.

James Henry said that he was Chardonnay's missing dad. Chardonnay had gone on a search for him and pleaded with him to back up her story. For all I knew, Chardonnay got some man to call so I could believe her lies. I asked James Henry to call Detective Wright and give him all and any information he had that could prove that Chardonnay was Prosperity's child.

He then told me a story that was even more interesting. He had no idea where Chardonnay had come from until recently, but after he found out that she came from my mother, he put two and two together. He told me that he was having an affair with my mom but did not think his wife knew about it. Once his wife found out, she approached my grandmother and mother about selling the child. My grandmother was agreeable because she did not want anything to interfere with her moneymaker. According to James Henry, he only recently found out this information and would be running a DNA test to verify that Chardonnay was his biological child. He also assured me that besides his wife, he had slept with no other woman but Prosperity.

I hung up the phone in total disbelief - not only disbelief about Chardonnay being my sister, but if she was my sister, how could she have been so evil? The minute she stepped into The Club, she had a vendetta against me. I just thought it was jealousy, and not once did I ever think it could have been revenge. I could not wait to find out what Detective Wright discovered as part of his investigation. Either way, what she had done was unforgivable, especially if we were family.

When I got home, Porchia was with another girl from school, preparing for their speech to their graduating class. From what I heard, it was going to be a dynamic speech. After her classmate left, she told me that Ravi, the Indian boy she had met at Georgetown, was coming to visit us. She was so excited and she went on and on about how I would love him. I was not sure about some stranger coming to stay with us. I asked Porchia what Ty had to say about that and she responded sarcastically, "Ty has been nothing but understanding." I was not certain exactly what that meant, but I guess I could go along with it as long as the boy was sleeping where I could see him.

Porchia's life was moving like a whirlwind and all I could do was watch. She was baptized, she bought a car, and she started hanging out with the young preacher from Better Hope Tabernacle. I liked him, but I liked Ty even more. I was not certain a preacher would be able to provide everything that my daughter deserved in life. Just observing them, it did not seem like Porchia was all that into him. I approached her about Pastor Sadiq and she pretty much blew me off.

"Why does everything have to be sexual with you, Mystery? We are just friends."

"Well, I can tell that he likes you beyond a friend. I see how he watches you."

"Only in your eyes. Man, I wish Aunt Hattie was here to put you in your place!"

"Why are you getting so defensive? I was just asking whether you had dumped Ty for the young pastor."

"I did not dump anyone for anybody. Just mind your own business."

"I am doing that. I just don't want you to get hurt."

"Too late," she responded and walked away.

I did not quite know how to take her comment but I felt that something was up between her and Ty. I knew it would do me no good to press her on the issue. We had fewer arguments these days and I wanted to keep it that way.

Porchia's Indian friend, Ravi, finally showed up. I was so impressed by the young man and the intelligence he showed toward any and all subjects. He even gave me some ideas about improving my business. It turned out that he traveled to different parts of Asia and he had an appreciation and understanding about adult entertainment. However, it totally shocked me when Ravi and Tracy became a couple. Tracy was a very simple girl without much motivation for doing much beyond shopping, movies, skating, and bowling. I don't think Tracy even thought about college at this point in her life. While Ravi was an intelligent, ambitious, well-traveled young man versed in many different areas, Tracy could not give an opinion about what was happening in the world if her life depended on it. I suppose opposites do attract.

Chapter 24

I was so busy with teenagers, graduation, Aunt Hattie's Retreat, and Sweezy that I was caught off guard when Detective Wright called and said he would like to see me in his office. I had just worked out, so I rushed over in my workout clothes, hoping that my deodorant was working well that day.

I walked in to find Detective Wright on the phone. He put his hand on the receiver and said, "Give me juth a minute."

I forgot about his speech impairment and knew that this would be a difficult conversation for both of us. He first confirmed that Chardonnay was definitely James Henry's daughter. He then went on to tell me that based on everything that he found, Chardonnay's story appeared to be true. He found some people who were aware of the relationship between my mother and James Henry. They also confirmed that my mother was pregnant before she had me, but no one knew what happened to the baby. Detective Wright said that to just make sure that we were sisters, we could take a DNA test. He informed me that we could take a sibling DNA test, but he had contacted the Maury Povich show and they were very interested in our story, and they would pay for the DNA test, our travel, and our lodging.

I was horrified that he would suggest that I would go and air our dirty secrets to all of America, I could not even respond to his suggestion. I said, "If I don't owe you anything else, I will be leaving and I sincerely appreciate your services."

He looked at me in shock and said, "I hope I did not offend you."

I stood up and said, "Offense taken."

I walked out of his office not knowing whether to scream or cry. How could that horrible person be my sister? I drove home, thinking about what I should do with the information. By the time I reached home, I decided to do nothing. I would not reach out to her and if she reached out to me, I would tell her that I was not interested in anything she had to say. My priority was where it had always been: making certain Porchia broke the DuBois Curse. That thought scared me because I realized that there may be another DuBois and the Curse might never be broken.

I passed by Aunt Hattie's Retreat before going home to pick up some papers out of my office. Sweezy was in the office with his head in his hands, leaning on the desk. He did not hear me enter the room.

"Hey baby, what's wrong?" I asked.

"Big John has just been diagnosed with Stage 3 Prostate Cancer."

"What?"

"Yeah, you know he never goes to the doctor. But he went to the doctor because he could not sleep at night because he pissed a lot. Then he started pissing blood. They examined him and told him that they would have to take a test. He took the test three days ago and was called in to the doctor's office to today to discuss treatment options."

"No, baby! This can't be happening."

"Mystery, he is in a good space. He said as long as he makes it to our wedding, he will be fine. But that is not okay for me."

"I know, baby. I feel the same way. Let's pray that the treatment options work."

"He said he did not want to do any radical treatment."

"What? Why?"

"I think he has not been happy since Cherelle committed suicide."

"What! Cherelle committed suicide?"

"Porchia never told you? 'Til this day, no one can mention suicide and Cherelle in the same sentence. We always have to say she died."

"Porchia knew?"

"Yeah, but Big John asked her not to say anything to anyone. And Mystery, please don't ever mention it."

"I won't, baby. This is just all a shock to me."

"That is why you are my queen."

"So what are we going to do about Big John?" I asked.

"We are going to make certain he does everything to live a long life."

"Sweezy, you know better than me how stubborn he is. Once he makes up his mind about something, there is no changing it."

"We are the dynamic duo. Working together, we can do anything."

I walked over to Sweezy and said, "Fiancé, I love you to death!"

Sweezy looked up and said, "Yeah, I am pretty loveable."

"Have you eaten lunch yet?" I asked.

"I am hungry, but only for you," he said.

"I am all funky. I just got through working out."

"Yeah, and I love you that way," Sweezy said.

Sweezy got up and locked the door and we made love right there on top of the desk.

We embraced quietly for a while after making love. I told Sweezy I had to leave but I would see him later on tonight, and we would figure out how best to take care of Big John.

"With you on my side, I can handle anything, Queen."

"Smooches. I will see you later."

When I walked to the main room I saw Chardonnay talking with the manager. I thought about trying to sneak out, but knew that one day I would have to face her.

I walked over and said, "Hey, Chardonnay, what brings you by?"

"Hello, Mystery. I was looking for you."

"How can I help you? I asked.

"Can we find a private place to talk?"

"I don't have time for you."

"Please, Mystery. I just want to talk with you."

I saw that she would not leave easily so I said, "Come. Follow me."

I led her to one of the spa rooms that was not currently occupied. She looked around as she was walking and said, "This is a nice spot, Mystery."

I ignored her comment and once we got into the room, I said, "Talk."

"Mystery, I just want to make up for everything I ever said or did. I want us to be family."

"It is too late for all of that. You have destroyed any chance of me wanting to be connected with you in any way."

"I have been attending church and I have repented from all my evil ways. I know what I did was wrong and unforgiveable. But if you could search your heart to forgive me, I will do everything in my power to make sure you do not have any regrets."

"I don't have any regrets now, Chardonnay. I have never done anything to you that you did not deserve. Did you know that at one time I almost thought about killing you?"

"No, but I understand why you would. But I want to leave you with something I discovered: Matthew 6:14-15. Just promise me you will read this verse and I will not contact you again."

"If that is all I have to do to get you to leave me and my family alone, I promise," I said.

As she left the room she looked back and said, "I love you, Mystery."

I could not believe she had the nerve to say "I", "love" and "Mystery" in the same sentence. I had not told Sweezy because I did not want anyone to know that this devil was any relation to me. I definitely did not want Porchia to have anything to do with her either. We were all moving in the right direction and I knew that Chardonnay was nothing but bad news.

I finally made it home to get out of my funky clothes, which were even more funked up by me being in the same room with Chardonnay. I took a long shower, just absorbing everything that had happened that day. When I got out of the shower, I decided to look up what Chardonnay gave me that would make her stay out of my life. I went and got Aunt Hattie's Bible from her room to look up the verses. It said, "For if ye forgive men their trespasses, your heavenly Father will also forgive you. But if ye forgive not men their trespasses, neither will your Father forgive your trespasses." The only trespass I knew about was when someone goes on your property without your permission. I was not certain what it meant in this context, but I would look it up later.

While sitting on Aunt Hattie's bed, I realized we had done nothing to Aunt Hattie's room since her death. Sometimes I noticed that Porchia would sleep in Aunt Hattie's bed. I don't know if that was her way of being close to Aunt Hattie, but I thought that we needed to do something. Aunt Hattie had a lot of clothes, hats, and shoes so I thought we probably could start there.

Porchia entered the house calling out my name. I hollered, "I am in Aunt Hattie's room."

"Why are you in here?" asked Porchia.

"Just thinking that we need to clean out this room."

"Why? It is not bothering anyone."

"Porchia, we can't just leave the room as if Aunt Hattie is coming back."

"This is my last connection to her, Mystery. Why are you trying to take that away?"

"I am not trying to take that away, but your connection lives in your heart, baby, not in a room."

Porchia screamed before leaving the room, "I will never forgive you if you change anything in this room!"

I thought to myself, *What a coincidence! I just read about forgiveness.*

Chapter 25

I remembered what happened between Emmit and I when I did not tell him that Porchia was my daughter. I did not want the same thing to happen with Sweezy. I thought it was important that we remained honest with each other. I met him at his house to speak about how we were going to help Big John. We decided that we would invite him over to the house for dinner and have a two-on-one conversation with him, hoping that we could convince him to take any measures he could to ensure that he lived. I would have Porchia research information about survival rates for those who had been diagnosed with Stage 3 prostate cancer. After we had our plan all set, I told him that I needed to tell him something.

His face dropped so I quickly said, "It's about Chardonnay."

"You are not thinking about killing her again, are you?"

"No, it is worse than that."

"What could be worse?"

"I found out that she is my sister."

Sweezy laughed and said, "Are you shitting me?"

"Sweezy, it is not funny."

"I am sorry, Queen. But you two are like Wolverine and Sabretooth."

"Sweezy, this is very upsetting to me. She scares me even more now that I know that we are sisters."

"Does Porchia know?"

"No, and I don't want her to know."

"Maybe she should. What if Chardonnay approaches her?"

"I never thought about that. But Chardonnay promised to stay away."

"And you believe that?"

"I don't know. She has not stayed away in the past."

"Well, history usually repeats itself," Sweezy said.

I looked at him and said, "I am going to look forward to the day that everything is good with me and those who I love."

"We will get there, Queen," Sweezy said, stroking my hair.

I laid my head on his shoulder and it felt so comfortable. How could a man seven years my junior make me feel so safe? I knew God would make certain that he stayed in my life forever.

***

Porchia's graduation day was perfect with the exception of Ty not being present. When I asked about Ty, Porchia simply said that he was trying to stay out of the limelight. I thought it was odd for him not to support his girlfriend on her graduation day. He was always there in the past and this was especially significant since she was giving the graduation speech.

Maybe he did not see it as important because he was already well beyond a high school graduation. Nonetheless, Porchia and her friend gave the best speech I have ever heard. They had the teachers, the students, and the attendees on their feet, clapping and snapping. I was so proud of my daughter. I just wished Aunt Hattie was here to see the fruits of her labor.

I wanted to take Porchia and her friends out for a graduation dinner, but they had plans of their own. So I made a date to take them to Pappa's Seafood after church on Sunday. The new minister gave an excellent sermon. He seemed to be the total opposite of Duke. It was totally understandable why Porchia would have a crush on him. However, I still thought that he could not offer her as much in life as Ty could.

We talked and laughed at dinner, but it seemed like Porchia did not have that same glee in her eye as she did when Ty was around. Ravi revealed during our dinner that he might stay in Houston to attend Rice University. It was apparent that he and Tracy were a couple. We had not seen him a lot since the night he met Tracy. Tracy was very happy, but Porchia seemed quite upset over the news. Her reaction was so out of character that I attempted to ease the tension by telling them I thought that love trumped all.

I still had not told Porchia about my engagement to Sweezy. I told Sweezy that I wanted to give Porchia a surprise birthday party and at the same time have a surprise engagement announcement. He thought that we should probably speak to Porchia prior to the public announcement, but he told me that he would leave it up to me. I wanted to make certain that all of Porchia's friends were present for her party, so I engaged Tracy to help me reach out to her friends. But, I took it upon myself to call Ty.

He answered the phone after the first ring and said, "Hi Mystery. Is everything okay?"

"Hi, Ty. Yes, just calling to invite you to Porchia's Surprise 18th birthday party."

"Does she know that you are inviting me?"

"No, silly. It is a surprise so I am not saying anything."

"I am sure this surprise will be priceless. What day and time?"

I gave him the information and asked him not to tell Porchia anything. He seemed more excited about her surprise party than I was about planning it. I was a little concerned about inviting Pastor Sadiq knowing that Ty would be there, but Porchia insisted that Sadiq was only a friend. I wanted everyone who loved my daughter to be there. I thought again about Aunt Hattie and was immediately saddened. I knew she would not be there physically, but would be with both of us in spirit on this important night.

I also planned another surprise for Porchia that I would give to her after the party. I had purchased our house from the owner and had quit-claimed the deed for the house to her. I knew she would be going away to school, but the way she acted when I said I wanted to clean Aunt Hattie's room, I knew she had a deep attachment not only to the room, but to the house. Sweezy and I discussed that I would move into his house after we married. I would give Porchia the choice of what she wanted to do with Aunt Hattie's house, while also letting her know that she was welcome to stay with us.

I was so glad that Ravi was around to help me do the shopping for the party. He also agreed to help me plan the party. He knew more about what Porchia would enjoy since they had been hanging out almost every day. It also gave me the opportunity to ask Ravi what was going on between Porchia and Ty.

"So Ravi, is Porchia and Ty still together?" I asked.

"I don't know much about what is going on with her and Ty."

"She has not said anything to you about him?"

"No. Not really," he responded.

"So what do you all talk about?"

"School. Life. Our futures," said Ravi.

"Does her future include Ty?"

"Mystery, I apologize, but I am uncomfortable talking about this with you. But you do know that Porchia is a very strong, intelligent, ambitious young woman. She will always do what she thinks is best."

Ravi did not directly answer my question, but he answered by not saying anything. Based on our conversation, I concluded that Porchia and Ty had broken up or were having problems. I did not want to interfere with her life, but I wanted to make certain that she was happy. I noticed that Porchia smiled a lot more when she spent time with Ty. I hoped that her birthday party would ignite some of the flames that they previously shared. I thought perhaps I would have a similar conversation with Tracy. But more than anything, I wished that Porchia shared her life with me the way she did with Aunt Hattie.

Chapter 26

Just when I thought I had done something right, Porchia made certain to let me know that I had fucked up once again. First, she was not happy about her surprise birthday party, although I saw her smiling a lot with Ty. Second, Sweezy was right. I should have told her privately about my engagement to Sweezy. When I announced that we were engaged, I was expecting her to be excited, but instead she stormed out of her party pouting. I tried to catch up with her for the next few days, but she was never around. I could not let her go off to college and not try to make things right. So one day I decided that I would stay home all day until I caught her.

I saw her walking up the sidewalk with her basketball in her hand. She looked surprised to see me sitting there. I apologized for not talking to her before I announced our engagement. I was as humble and honest as I could be. She pretty much dismissed my apology and went on about her business. I immediately called Sweezy after she went into the house.

"Sweezy, she will never speak to me again."

"What are you talking about, Mystery?"

"Porchia just told me that I was a gold-digger and I did not love you, that I was only taking advantage of you. And that she would pray for me."

"Queen, she is just upset. You know how Swoosh gets. She uses words as a weapon."

"No, she was serious. I can't lose her now."

"You won't lose her. She is just hurt. I will talk with her."

"Will you do that?"

"Yes. I love Swoosh and want her to be part of our lives."

"Thank you, Sweezy. Thank you so much."

"Don't thank me. It's my obligation to keep our family together."

"Well, can I tell you I love you?" I asked.

"Always and forever," he said.

"Okay. I will see you later on," I said.

I don't know what I did to have such a great man in my life. But I knew at that moment that I would do everything in my power to make certain I kept a smile on his face.

Sweezy caught up with Porchia a few days later. He said everything was cool and we would all be okay. Sweezy also told me that he had caught Porchia getting ready for a date.

He said, "Yeah, she was all dressed up and wearing some pearls that I had given Chanti."

"Was she waiting for Ty?"

"I did not feel like I should be asking questions since I was trying to apologize."

"Sweezy, you should have. I don't know what is going on with her?"

"Well, she seemed anxious to get me out of the house."

"You should have talked to her longer to see who it was!"

"See, Queen, that is your problem. You don't give her enough space."

"I give her a lot of space."

"You need to let her feel comfortable with you. She will let you know in due time."

"What, when I am old and gray and hard of hearing?"

Sweezy laughed. "You know, Queen, you can be so dramatic. But I love you anyway."

"Since you think I am too pushy, I will let you be the one to get the scoop and feed it to me. I would ask Aunt Hattie to do the same thing, but I knew she did not tell me everything. But I know my loving husband will tell me everything."

"Oh you know, huh?"

"Yes, 'cause I will cut you off if you don't."

As Sweezy predicted, Porchia started talking to me again. I was able to tell her about the house. She was exceedingly happy and she told me that I did a very "selfless" thing. I was so used to selfish and was not certain what a selfless thing was. I assumed it was good because she was smiling as she said it. She also shared with me that she had decided to attend a seminary school instead of going to Georgetown. I must say that

I was a little disappointed that she would not be pursuing a higher-paying career, but I realized it was her decision and her life. The best thing I could do is support her through this time.

She also told me that she and Ty had broken up. She did not get into all of the details, but she said that it was an amicable break-up and they had agreed to remain friends. I noticed that she had started hanging out with Pastor Sadiq more these days. She told me that she was not serious about anybody at this particular time in her life. She was happy that she had found her direction in life and she would be open to all opportunities. I did not necessarily agree with everything that she said or did, but she seemed to be very sure of herself. I had not seen her demonstrate such confidence in a long time. I knew that she would not fall victim to the DuBois Curse.

Despite Porchia and I having a better relationship and more candid discussions, I could not help feeling that she still did not approve of my relationship with Sweezy. I wondered whether she still felt that I was just using him. We seemed to be in a good space so I brought up the subject of our wedding to see how she would respond.

"Porchia, will you be my maid of honor for our wedding?"

"I was wondering when you would ask again. Hopefully, this time it happens."

"Are you okay with me marrying Sweezy?"

"Mystery, I have been watching the two of you. I have never seen two people get along so well. I could not do anything but support the two of you. Sweezy has smiled more than I have ever seen him smile. And you seem to be happier than I have ever seen you. Even when I try to upset you, you are still happy. What God has brought together, let no man separate."

I could not control the tears flowing from my eyes. Porchia put her arms around me and said, "I thought you would be happy that I am happy for you."

"Porchia, beside your birth, this is one of the happiest days of my life."

"Now I set all of this up to ask you for a favor," said Porchia.

"Anything," I responded.

"Uh, don't open yourself up like that. You know the old Porchia would have told you to take a one-way trip to hell," she said, laughing.

"Yeah, but I know that I am dealing with a new and improved Porchia."

"Ha! I don't know about new and improved, but I'm just trying to follow Jesus's example."

"I have always wondered about your transformation."

"I had to follow the Light."

"The Light?" I asked.

Porchia laughed and said, "It is a long story. One day we will sit with a glass of wine and I will tell you all about it. But what I would like to know is whether you would come with me to Durham to find a place to live?"

"I am mentally packing right now," I said.

"Can you leave this weekend?"

"Anything for you, my love."

"Well if that is the case, can I have $40,000?" Porchia asked.

Knowing that she was joking, I said, "Look, don't push it."

Chapter 27

I was so excited when Porchia asked me to go with her to North Carolina to find a place to live. We arrived at Raleigh-Durham airport and I was impressed. I thought it was going to be a very small airport, but it was bigger than Hobby. I just knew that Houston had the worst humidity, but walking outside of the airport, I could have sworn I walked into a steam room. My hair instantly stuck to my head. Porchia immediately pulled her long black hair up into a scrunchie and looked at me and said, "I need a shower now."

We arrived at our hotel and Porchia looked at me and asked whether we had to fight over the shower. We both laughed, remembering the time she had pushed me into the bathtub. Her story slightly differed from mine. As she tells the story, she barely brushed my shoulder. I told her that I would shank her to get into the shower before her.

She laughed and said, "My God will hunt you down because I have some serious work to do for Him."

It was interesting watching Porchia as she developed an intimate relationship with God. It was clear to me that nothing and no one would get in her way of following what she felt she had to do.

We found a cute apartment near Duke Divinity School. Porchia even took me to meet the head of her department, which I found out later was a friend of Pastor Sadiq. We had a very interesting conversation with Professor Minet, pronounced Min-yay. She spoke very highly of Pastor Sadiq and I could see Porchia blushing as she spoke about him. It made me wonder whether there was more to their relationship than friendship. I guess Porchia would tell me when the time was right, but I could see brightness in her eyes when she spoke about him.

I was anxious to help Porchia furnish her place so we could both take a trip to Charlotte. After getting over our disappointment that there was no Ikea in the Raleigh-Durham area, we hit the streets of Durham in search of furniture. Luckily, we ran into a person that guided us to a place that was similar to Ikea, and we were able to find Porchia everything she needed. After getting her situated, I asked her if she would mind taking a trip with me to Charlotte.

"That is cool. That is one city that I would like to see. But why do you want to go?"

"Well, Sweezy and I had been looking at other cities outside of Texas to bring our concept of Aunt Hattie's Retreat," I answered.

"Oh, y'all trying to do it big. Dallas and Austin are not big enough."

"Well, you know we already started building one in Atlanta. Why not hit up Charlotte?"

"I am not mad at you. I am your beneficiary. It is all good," Porchia said, laughing.

"I am going to leave my money to the Tree Huggers Organization in Berkeley," I said, snickering.

We drove a little over two hours to Charlotte to meet with a real estate agent who reminded me of the importer-exporter that I met on suggardaddie.com. However, this man was much rounder and shorter. He drove us in his pickup truck to spots where I was scared to get out. They looked like demolished buildings that would have been located in the Ninth Ward of New Orleans after Hurricane Katrina. I could tell that Porchia was getting irritated.

When we arrived at the third place, Porchia said, "Pardon me, sir. Have you ever heard of George Jefferson?"

The real estate agent looked confused and said, "On the TV show?

"Yes sir. In case you have not heard, we have moved on up. What is this junk you are showing us?"

That child of mine may have found Jesus, but she still did not mince her words.

I interrupted Porchia before she said something else. "We appreciate your time. We have had a very long day. Perhaps we can start again tomorrow morning. I would be interested in seeing locations near city center."

"But I thought you were opening a strip club? Strip clubs do better in the hood," he responded.

I was so upset I forgot the man's name and pulled a Porchia and said, "Look, Barney, you are not the agent for us. Please drive us back to the hotel so we can end this nightmare."

The ride back to the hotel would have been quiet with the exception of Porchia playing rap music loudly on her phone without the headset. I wanted to crack up because I knew Porchia did not like rap music. When Lil John's song came on, she started shouting, "Turn down for what!" It was the extended version, so this went on for at least five minutes. I looked over at the bald, fat agent and he was looking straight ahead with both hands on the wheel. By the time we arrived at the hotel, I was deaf and the real estate agent was petrified.

Porchia and I got out of the truck laughing so hard that I thought I would pee on myself.

I looked at Porchia and said, "Now that was not God-like."

She winked at me and said, "God ain't through with me yet!"

I called Sweezy when we got into our room to tell him about our adventure. Sweezy asked to speak to Porchia. I am not certain what he was saying, but she was laughing the entire conversation. She ended with, "That's wrong! But I will remember that. Here is yo' girl," she said, laughing and handing the phone back to me.

I said, "I guess you two have inside jokes."

"We were just remembering some thangs. Queen, I have some real estate contacts for you. I have peeps in Charlotte."

"Why did you make me go through that if you have contacts?"

"Life would be boring without adventures."

"Yeah, you better remember that when I give you drama."

"I am looking forward to it."

"You say that now. Well, Porchia and I have not eaten so we need to find something to eat."

"Okay. I miss you."

"Miss you more. I will call you later on tonight."

"Will be waiting."

Porchia suggested we go work out before eating. I thought it was a good idea because I had not worked out in a while. We walked into the gym and there he was standing there and looking at the weights. Porchia looked at me and I shrugged my shoulders.

"Ty! What are you doing here?" asked Porchia.

He walked over to us and said, "Hello. It's nice to see both of you." He hugged Porchia and kissed me on the cheek.

I said, "This is a surprise."

"I am here because I am a groomsman in my friend's wedding. He plays for the Panthers. What are you doing here?" he asked.

I answered, "I am looking for another city to open up Aunt Hattie's Retreat."

"This would be an excellent location," said Ty.

"Well, we don't want to interrupt your workout, Ty," said Porchia.

"You could never be an interruption to me. I am just glad to see you."

"Well, as you see, I have added a couple of pounds so I have to go get my workout on," said Porchia.

"You always look good to me, Pocahontas."

I walked over to the treadmill while Porchia headed to the elliptical. I could see her eyeing Ty and thought to myself, *She still has feelings for him. The thrill is not gone.* We worked out for about an hour and Ty was also still pretending to work out. He was pretending to work out because he was eyeing Porchia most of the time. I thought to myself, *I don't know what happened between them, but it is obvious that they still have feelings for one another.*

When Ty saw that we were through working out, he walked over and asked, "So what are you two getting into?"

"We are going to shower then head out to dinner," I said. I saw from the corner of my eye that Porchia was rolling her eyes at me.

"I would love to take you both to dinner if it is okay with you?"

"That sounds good, huh, Porchia?"

I could feel Porchia's eyes piercing through me, but she said, "Sure."

"Okay. I will meet you both in the lobby in an hour," said Ty.

Porchia looked at me, then Ty, and said, "Princess will not be ready in an hour. She needs at least an hour and a half."

Ty laughed and said, "Okay, see you then."

When Ty left, Porchia looked at me and said, "You will die a painful death."

"Stop playing. I saw you checking him out. He is even finer now," I said.

"Ms. Sweezy, you better stop checking out other men."

"I am trying to hook you up. It would be great to see you as happy as I am. Maybe we can have a double wedding."

Porchia responded, "Only in your dreams! Be thankful that I agreed to be your maid of honor."

I thought I would leave it alone and let God's plan reveal itself.

Chapter 28

Ty, Porchia, and I had a great dinner and went out to a club afterwards. They danced while I was being bought drinks by wannabe suitors. Every time they would come to the table, I turned them and their drinks away. But I was very gracious about it. I told them I appreciated their southern hospitality, but my husband was on the floor dancing with my sister. I was enjoying seeing my baby enjoy herself. I wondered if Ty's number was the same because we needed to have another chat.

I found a potential spot for mine and Sweezy's next business venture. I was looking forward to my next trip to Charlotte with him. This was exciting because it meant that I could spend a lot of time with Porchia by opening up a business in Charlotte. By the time we left for Houston, we had the apartment completely together. I was so glad that she was not staying yet because I would have broken down. I could not imagine what it would be like when she left. I had never been without my baby more than a week at a time. I made up my mind that I would lead the Charlotte project and I would have to convince Sweezy that hands-on supervision was needed.

After we spent time with Ty, I noticed Porchia's attitude had changed. Any time I asked about Ty, she would shut me down. Perhaps I would try again to see what really happened between them and see if she would give him another chance.

We were on the plane and she was staring out of the window.

"Porchia, is everything okay?"

"Yeah, why do you ask?"

"It seems like your mind is elsewhere."

"Uh, yeah. I am starting a new life in a new place."

"But you said that you were sure this was your destiny."

"It is, Mystery, but that does not mean that I am not scared."

"You will do just fine. Would it be okay if I stay with you once I start the new business?" I asked.

"Yeah, that is why I got two bedrooms."

"It was nice seeing you happy spending time with Ty."

"Where are you going with this, Mystery?"

"I am just saying. You looked happy like you used to when he was around."

"Well, he is not around anymore. The only relationship I am trying to kindle is my relationship with God."

"Girl, God will not be there to hold you at night."

"Mystery, He is my comforter day and night."

"But you know that is not the same."

"You are right. It is not the same, but better."

"You are so stubborn."

"And so are you. Can we please not talk about Ty anymore?"

"Okay. I just want to see you happy."

"I will be. Speaking of happy, are all the plans for the wedding set?"

"Yes. I can't wait! Two weeks seem too long to wait to be Mrs. Sylvester Stone."

Porchia laughed loudly and said, "Sweezy's real name is Sylvester?"

"Oooh, do not tell him I told you that!"

"That is hella funny! What black person names their child Sylvester?"

"That is a story for another day. So when will you leave for Durham?"

"I plan to return a week after the nuptials."

"Porchia, why don't you go with us on our honeymoon to Bora Bora?"

"I am not accompanying my mom and stepdad on their honeymoon! That is the craziest idea I have ever heard from you."

"No, it will be fun."

"No, Mystery!"

"Okay. I thought that we could just spend time together on a beautiful island before you leave," I said.

"Negative. That won't be happening. But we can plan another vacation together."

When we arrived back in Houston, I still had a lot to accomplish for the ceremony. I hired another wedding consultant, but no one could make my day perfect but me. We had 500 guests attending. But the most important guest was Big John. We had convinced him to follow the doctor's advice and let them operate and treat with radiation. He was staying with us and recovering well. It seemed that he would be ready to stand as Sweezy's best man at our wedding.

I was anxious for the date night I planned with Sweezy upon my return. I had some exciting news to share with him, and I wanted to show him just how much I missed him. I contacted Ms. Marvelle before I left Durham to have her plan our special night. When we landed, I dropped Porchia off at the house and drove to Vicky's Promise to find the right lingerie for the occasion. When I got there, guess who was working at the shop? Yes, my evil sister Chardonnay.

She seemed genuinely happy to see me. She went out of her way to help me find the perfect outfit and also let me use her employee discount. She congratulated me on my wedding and told me that she wished me nothing but happiness. I felt bad when I left because as much as she tried to be nice, I did not trust her further than I could see her. It also reminded me that I had not told Porchia about Chardonnay - first thing on my to-do list after my special date night with Sweezy.

When I arrived at Sweezy's house, he was not there. I spent time talking with Big John. He confided in me that he really felt like he did not have anything to live for after the wedding.

"Big John, that is so far from the truth. You have your whole life ahead of you."

"It has not been the same for me since I lost Cherelle. I am just so glad that Sweezy found you. You have made a big difference in his life. No one deserves to feel the way I do."

"But you have to be around for your grandchildren."

"What grandchildren?"

"I did not want to say anything, but I am pregnant."

"How did that happen, Mystery?"

"Do I need to explain that to you, Big John?" I said, laughing.

"Does Sweezy know?"

"No, this is what this night is all about."

"Congratulations! I did not think you wanted any more children. But I think both of you will make great parents."

"Blame it on the birth control. But I am happy."

"Well, I am going out to get out of your way."

"You are not in our way, Big John."

"I just need some time alone. Tell Sweezy I will see him later. I need for both of you to know that I love you as if you were my own children. I appreciate all that you have done."

"I know that Big John. And we love you too."

My evening with Sweezy was perfect: the meal, the lighting, the Jacuzzi, the lingerie, and the lovemaking.

We were both lying on our backs and looking at the moon from the bedroom patio door.

I rolled over toward him and said, "I need to tell you something."

"What is it, Queen?"

"What do you think about us having kids?"

"I often think about that once we get everything operational and we are semi-retired."

"Sweezy, semi-retired? I don't want kids in my old age."

"No, I am talking in about five years. I don't want anyone but us raising our children and we are way too busy right now to properly raise children."

"I will be almost thirty-five in five years."

"The new thirty-five is like twenty-five. You heard?"

"Not for my body. The older you get, the more difficult it is to have kids."

"We just need one."

"Sweezy, I am sorry, but we are having one in nine months."

"What did you say?"

"I am pregnant!"

Sweezy got up without saying anything, dressed, and then left the house.

Chapter 29

I couldn't believe that another man had broken off an engagement. Sweezy acted as if I planned to get pregnant. Pregnancy was the furthest thing from my mind. My choice for birth control was the Depo shot and it worked for years. None of that mattered because I was determined that I would raise my baby alone, just like I did Porchia, but this time it would be without Aunt Hattie. I was happy about the pregnancy and I would have told Porchia, but I felt obligated to tell Sweezy first. My happiness quickly turned to doom thinking about all of the bad news that I had to share with Porchia.

When I arrived back home, Porchia was not there. I headed to the bathroom to take a shower, but before getting into the shower, I heard the doorbell ring. I could not imagine who would have been ringing the doorbell at that hour. I went to the door in my robe and could see that Sweezy's car was parked outside.

I let him in and he grabbed me and said, "We will work this out. I love you and I will love our baby."

"Sweezy, you just left me. How could you do that?"

"I was in shock, Queen. I did not want to say the wrong thing. I just needed time to think it all out."

"So every time you need to think about what to say, you will just leave?"

"No. This is a game-changer. I was looking forward to just you and me doing our thing. But it is not in the cards that way. It is you, me, and Junior."

"It may be a girl, Sweezy."

"She still will be Junior."

I laughed and kissed him and asked him whether he was sure. He told me he would not have it any other way.

As we were hugging, Porchia walked in and said, "Are you two having a lovefest right in the middle of the living room?"

I looked at Sweezy, then at Porchia, and said, "Too late for a lovefest, but we have some news for you."

"Should I sit down first?" asked Porchia.

"Yeah, let's all sit down," said Sweezy.

Sweezy and I sat on the sofa. Porchia sat in Aunt Hattie's chair with her long legs crossed underneath her and looked at us and asked, "What's up?"

I hesitated before answering but Sweezy jumped in and said, "Mystery got us pregnant!"

I slapped Sweezy on the back of his neck and said, "Yeah, I did it all alone."

"Wait. Y'all having a baby?" Porchia asked.

"Yep. Sweezy Junior," said Sweezy.

"I am going to have a little brother?"

"No, we don't know yet, Porchia. Sweezy is just being wishful," I said.

"Well, I think it would be great to have a little sister or brother. I have always been lonely growing up as the only child in the house," said Porchia.

"Girl, you mean spoiled as the only child," I said.

"Yeah, that too," laughed Porchia. "I can't believe how my family has grown over the last year! A mother, a stepfather, three sisters, two brothers and another sibling on the way. We can have a real Thanksgiving dinner now," said Porchia.

"Well, you might as well add an aunt to that list," I said.

Sweezy looked at me and then at Porchia and said, "This is my cue to leave. I have some things to do at the house. I love you both."

Sweezy gave me a kiss and whispered "good luck" in my ear. He then went to kiss Porchia on the head and departed.

"Why did Sweezy just leave like the po-po's were after him?" asked Porchia.

"Do you remember that lady that came by the house that you were talking to when I arrived?" I asked.

"Yeah, that nice lady named Zinfandel?" Porchia asked.

I laughed and said, "Chardonnay."

"Yeah. I knew it was some wine. So what about her?"

"Well, I recently found out that my mother had another baby before I was born and she is that baby."

"You gotta be kidding, Mystery!" said Porchia.

"I wish I was," I responded.

"Why? Don't you like the idea of having a sister?" asked Porchia.

"Well, I hope it grows on me," I responded.

I did not want to go into everything that Chardonnay had done. There was no reason to have Porchia upset about history. I wanted to look forward to our future in a positive way. I thought if I nurtured positivity, positivity might nurture me. No more wondering why bad things were happening. I would celebrate the good things and hopefully learn a lesson from the bad things.

Porchia looked at me and said, "I think that our family will only grow stronger within the next year."

I walked over to her and said, "That is my prayer also, baby. I just wish Aunt Hattie could see us now."

Porchia looked up at me and said, "She does."

As the big date approached, although I would remain positive, I decided to also be proactive. I called Pastor Sadiq and told him that we were writing our own vows and I wanted him to skip the part that asked the crowd if anybody disagreed with our marriage. I did not want to invite any drama to our wedding. He told me that he would like to schedule me and Sweezy for our mandatory counseling session. I told him I forgot about it and asked him if we could skip it. He told me absolutely not. I set a session for us that day. I hoped I could get Sweezy to attend because I forgot to tell him about this requirement for Pastor Sadiq to marry us. I called Sweezy right away.

Sweezy answered his phone, "What's up, Queen?"

"Hey, baby. Are you doing anything at five today?"

"I am taking Big John for a treatment at three o'clock but we should be done by then."

"Cool. We have to go to a counseling session."

"Mystery, I said everything was fine. I am good. I love you. I will always love you. We get along just fine. What do we need counseling for?"

"It is mandatory for Pastor Sadiq to marry us."

"What does he know about marriage? He ain't neva been married!"

"I know, baby, but it is a requirement."

"He is wasting our time. But okay, I will do it. Can I just meet you there?"

"Yeah, no problem. I will see you then. Love you," I said.

"Always and forever," said Sweezy.

Chapter 30

I met Pastor Sadiq at his office at the church. He told me it was nice to see me and asked me about Sweezy. I ensured him that Sweezy was on his way. After twenty minutes, I became concerned. I excused myself from Pastor Sadiq's office to call Sweezy. There was no answer. I called right back and my call went to voicemail. I left a message that said, "Sweezy, did you forget that we were meeting with Pastor Sadiq? Please call me as soon as you get this message."

I walked back into Pastor Sadiq's office and told him I wasn't certain what happened, but maybe we should reschedule. He looked at me and said, "Mystery, don't worry. I am sure everything is okay. Call me to reschedule."

It caught me off guard that he read my mind. I was very concerned because this was not like Sweezy. He would never stand me up.

After leaving Pastor Sadiq's office, I called Porchia to ask her if she had heard from Sweezy and she told me no. I called Big John's phone and there was no answer. I decided to drive out to the house to see if Sweezy was there. Ms. Marvelle answered the door and

I ran in, asking her if she had seen Sweezy. She told me that she had not seen him since earlier in the afternoon. I started walking in circles and Ms. Marvelle asked me what was wrong. I told her that Sweezy was supposed to show up for a pre-marital counseling session and he never showed or called. She tried to calm me down, but it upset me more.

I screamed out, "Something is wrong, Ms. Marvelle. I can feel it!"

I went to Sweezy's office and called the hospitals, the morgue, and the jails to check if he was in one of those places. About two hours after Sweezy had gone MIA, Sweezy called my phone. When I answered it and he hesitated to speak, I immediately knew something was wrong.

"Baby, what's wrong?" I heard a whimper. "Sweezy are you there?"

"I am."

"Where are you?"

"I don't know."

I realized that he was drunk. "Sweezy, have you been drinking?"

No answer.

"Baby, are you okay?"

"No, I am not. Big John left us."

"What?"

"He is gone, Mystery," Sweezy said in almost a whisper.

"Baby, where are you? I will come get you."

"No. I am not in a good way. I will talk with you tomorrow."

"Sweezy!"

No answer. He had ended the call.

I sat there for a while in disbelief. I did not understand what happened to Big John. He seemed to be doing well. And why did Sweezy insist on being alone? We should be grieving together.

I told Ms. Marvelle and she seemed to take the news hard, but she asked me what she could do for me. I told her that I would be fine, but to call me the minute Sweezy arrived home. She assured me that she would, so I left. As I drove off, I started to wonder whether I was the one cursed. I pulled the car to the side of the road to have a discussion with God. I asked Him to protect my loved ones from future harm. I asked Him to show me the way to prevent harm from happening to people around me. I told Him that I was confused and I did not know what else to do. I asked God to help me.

I arrived home and when I walked in, the lights came on and everyone yelled, "Surprise!"

Porchia was smiling and she ran toward me and said, "I told you I would get you back! But people were almost leaving. Why are you so late?"

I just looked at her and tears began rolling down my cheeks.

Porchia said, "Oh, Mystery, I did not expect tears."

"I can't do this, Porchia." I ran past everyone into my room.

Porchia came in a few seconds later and said, "What's wrong, Mystery?"

"Big John is dead and I don't know where Sweezy is."

"Okay. I will be back. Let me go tell Tracy what happened so she can get rid of everybody."

Porchia walked back into the room a few minutes later. "Mystery, what happened?"

"I don't know, Porchia."

"Are you okay?"

"No, I am not. Big John was like a father to both of us. Now Sweezy is missing. No, I am not okay. I don't understand any of this. Just when things could be right for us, everything goes wrong."

"Mystery, I am so sorry. I have a difficult time with death also, but I have come to realize it is part of the bigger plan. The minute we are born, the minute we are closer to death. What is important is that we develop a strong relationship with God so that we can live abundantly here on earth. And the good news is that God has promised us everlasting life if we accept Jesus."

"Porchia, my question to God is, why have I been cursed? So many bad things have happened to me during my life. It would be nice just to have things right some time."

"Mystery, I don't want to sound harsh, but there are some things you must change."

"Go on, Porchia, say what you have to say. It can't be worse than when you called me whore, tramp, and bitch most of my life."

"I was so out of line for that. I do apologize. But you spend entirely too much time pouting about things that are not working instead of thanking God for your blessings. Yes, you have experienced things during your life that a young child should never have experienced, but God has brought you through all of that. You had a loving woman to take care of both you and your young child, you are a successful businesswoman, you are about to marry the man of your dreams, and you have been blessed with the opportunity to raise another child. From my viewpoint, you have risen above all of your circumstances. God has truly shown you favor."

I wondered how my child could make such sense. I was spending a lot of time saying "why me" instead of thanking God for his blessings. I hugged Porchia and said, "Thank you. Thank you for your words. Thank you for being you. Thank you for the surprise bridal shower. Do you think people are still here?" I asked.

"I asked Tracy to apologize and asked her to thank them for their attendance and their gifts. But let's go out and see," said Porchia.

"Let me pull myself together and I will be right out," I said.

I went to the bathroom and looked in the mirror and said, "From this day on, I will praise you, God, for getting me through both the good and bad times." I saw a glow in my face that I had never seen before. I splashed some water on my face then wiped it down. I had no makeup on and this was the first time I realized I did not need makeup. I realized at that moment that God could wash all of our flaws away. I smiled at myself, lifted my shoulders, and walked out to see who was still present for my bridal shower.

I walked out and was sort of relieved to see it was primarily family, Tracy, Ms. Carletta and her mother, and Chardonnay. I almost fell out to see that Chardonnay was present. I greeted everyone and apologized for my absence from the party. I found Porchia and asked her why she had invited Chardonnay. She looked at me, confused, and said, "She is family too." I realized I did not tell Porchia everything so I just smiled and said, "You are right."

I walked over to Chardonnay and said, "Hi there. Surprised to see you."

"My niece invited me and I was happy to accept," Chardonnay said, smiling.

"I thought we agreed to no contact," I said.

"I just wanted to share in your happy moment."

"Well, can you do me a favor?" I asked.

"Sure," responded Chardonnay.

"Let me invite you before you accept."

"Okay, but Porchia said it was a surprise so I could not get your permission. She also told me that you had told her everything. I just assumed it was okay to come," Chardonnay said.

"It's okay. As long as we understand each other," I said.

"I understand that you have not forgiven me yet. Hopefully one day you will. I apologize for any problem I have caused you. Congratulations again," Chardonnay said.

Chardonnay went over to Porchia and said something to her, they kissed, and she left.

I just could not trust Chardonnay yet. She was acting as if she had changed, but she was probably trying to gain my trust to stab me in the back again. I thought I should also caution Porchia about trusting Chardonnay.

I sat with the remainder of my family and opened gifts. We laughed at some of the outfits. Ms. Carletta, by far, had bought the kinkiest outfit. It was a black sheer top with a garter belt and fishnet stockings. We all laughed until she said, "There is more." I then pulled out handcuffs and a whip.

Everyone gasped and Porchia shouted out, "Oh no! Ms. Carletta is a closet freak!"

We all fell out laughing. We sat around talking and laughing for another hour. When everyone left, I breathed a sigh of relief. I was grateful that they had come out for me, but at the same time, I was worried about Sweezy. I had not heard from him or Ms. Marvelle.

I wanted so badly to drink some wine to calm myself down, but I could not do so because of the little one in my tummy. Oh, what I would have done for some of Aunt Hattie's teacakes and some warm milk! Instead, I poured a glass of apple juice and called it a night. I felt my eyes getting heavy so I called Sweezy, but he did not answer. I said a prayer for him, lay down, and drifted off to sleep.

I woke up the next morning startled. Someone was lying next to me with his arms around my waist. I turned over slowly to see Sweezy peacefully sleeping. A calming feeling rushed throughout my body. I just stared at him for a while and smiled. I tried to gently get up without waking him, but he stirred when I moved.

He looked up at me and said, "Good morning, Queen. I hope I did not worry you."

I just kissed him and told him I was glad that he was okay. I looked at my phone and Ms. Marvelle had called a couple of times. I looked at Sweezy and said, "I have to go to the bathroom and you need to call Ms. Marvelle."

He said, "I am a lucky man to have so many women worried about me. Porchia left me a message last night telling me to get my butt over here because you were worried sick. She said she was concerned about me, you, and the baby. So I came right over after she left that message. You were snoring, so I crept into the bed because I did not want you to wake up punching."

"Please stop running away," I said.

"I am. I will only run to you from now on out, Queen."

"Will you go with me to counseling?" I asked.

"Yes, I think that is a good idea."

"Not just for our wedding, but after that," I said. "We have had a lot going on and I think talking about it would be good."

"You know I love you, right?" I asked.

"Always and forever," Sweezy responded.

"Okay. I have to use the bathroom. Call Ms. Marvelle now!"

Chapter 31

Sweezy later told me why he was so upset. Big John had not died from prostate cancer, but from heartbreak. He explained that he had arrived at Big John's house to take him to his treatment but he did not answer, so he used his key to get into the house. He walked in to find Big John dead in his bedroom with a gun near his body. Big John had left a note with both of our names on it. Sweezy handed me the note to read. It read: "Sweezy, I don't want to be a burden to you anymore. You should be able to live without worrying about taking care of me. You have grown into a man that I am proud to have fathered. I am asking that you don't give me a funeral. Please cremate my body. I don't want people pretending to like me and my body being on display. I have liquated all of my assets and put it in Chase Bank and you are the sole beneficiary. Use the money wisely. I hope you understand my reasons behind this. We have talked many times about how I feel that life is not worth it since I lost Cherelle. I thought with time, it would get better, but it has actually gotten worse. I am sorry I did not get to say bye, but I believe this is the best way. I have done this not out of pity, but out of love. I want you to live your life happily with Mystery. She is a good woman and I believe she is the woman for you. Don't run away, but run to her when things get rough. She can help you through the difficult times. Mystery is like the daughter I never had and I am leaving it up to you to take care of her and your baby. I could not love a biological son more that I love you. Make me proud son."

I looked at Sweezy and said, "I am not certain I can go on reading this."

"Did you read what he wrote to you?" Sweezy asked.

"No. I stopped with yours."

"Well, he made a specific request to you."

I wiped my tears and kept reading. It read: "Mystery, I remember a little withdrawn teenage girl walking into The Club and I knew that you had something I had never seen in a child. I could see pain, but I also saw ambition and success. You did not prove me wrong. You have blossomed into a very beautiful, intelligent woman who knows what she wants and how to get it. But relax and enjoy life. Please learn how to let Sweezy take care of you. I know that you have been used to taking care of everything and everybody around you. I want you to experience everything that life has to offer. Stop worrying about Porchia. She has so much of you in her she will be able to survive anything. I know you will make a great mother to your new baby. You and Sweezy will have enough from my assets that you will never have to work again. I know that will be unacceptable to you, but please stop to smell the roses. Be good to yourself and your family. I told Sweezy no funeral services. I am asking you to make certain that he follows my request. I never traveled to the Grand Canyon. Cherelle and I often talked about taking that trip. I would like for my ashes to be spread across the Grand Canyon. I am sorry that I did not wait for the wedding, but another day living would have been a day too long. I hope you understand my reasons for what I have done. You are probably saying I said more in death than I did in life. I was not one for a lot of words, but deeds. I hope my deeds showed my love for you. In parting, I am wishing you a lifetime of happiness. I love you, Moneymaker."

I could not control my tears. If Sweezy had not been holding me the entire time, I don't know whether I would have been able to handle what I read. Even after reading the letter, I was still not certain why Big John took his life. I was always taught that this was the ultimate sin. If you killed yourself, you could not inherit the kingdom of God. If he loved Cherelle as much as I thought he did, he would not be reunited with her. And how could he leave Sweezy? He was going to be Sweezy's best man at the funeral. I don't care what Big John said in his letter. I thought it was a very selfish act.

I looked at Sweezy and muttered between my tears, "Baby, I don't want to go through with the wedding."

"Queen, what are you saying?"

"Let's elope. Let's you, me, and Porchia go to Las Vegas with Big John's ashes to marry. Then we can take a trip to the Grand Canyon to spread his ashes."

"But you wanted a big wedding."

"I can't do it now, baby. It will be too hard for you."

Sweezy sighed and said, "I want to make you happy and if having a wedding makes you happy, I am willing to do it."

"No, Sweezy, having a wedding won't make me happy. Being your wife will make me happy. I don't need a big ceremony for that."

Sweezy looked at me and said, "Let's leave as soon as possible."

"Let me check with Porchia to see how soon she would be able to leave," I said.

"Cool."

"Sweezy, I hope I can share with Porchia what happened."

"Yeah. She kept how Cherelle died a secret, so I know she would do the same for Big John. Do you want me to tell her?" Sweezy asked.

"No. I have kept so many things from her in the name of love and trying to protect her. When I look back, I was probably only protecting myself. I want to turn over a new leaf by being honest with her."

"You are an amazing woman and mother. I want no other woman to be the mother of my children."

"Children? Slow your role, partna. We have to concentrate on this one," I said, rubbing my belly.

"You acting like your eggs are going to dry up, so I thought we would make the best of it."

"Keep talking, buddy, and you will not get a chance to ever get near my dried-up eggs again."

I spoke to Porchia about our plans to elope to Vegas and told her that we wanted her to come. She, of course, started asking why we were changing our plans after we had invested so much in our wedding. I explained to Porchia what happened to Big John. She was visibly shaken by the news to the point that she started crying. She started talking about Cherelle and Chanti and how suicide was never an answer. She viewed Big John as invincible and found it difficult to understand why he would take his own life. I wondered about Porchia's view about suicide and whether they would be able to go to heaven.

"Porchia, so do you believe that a person who kills himself can inherit the kingdom of God?"

"God wants us all to value life, not only others', but our own. One of the Ten Commandments states that one should not kill. It does state that you should not kill another or one's self. But many have said that this applies to killing of others. But even if this definition is expanded to killing others and yourself, disobeying a commandment within itself does not prevent one from inheriting the kingdom."

"So are you saying that a person who commits suicide can go to heaven?" I asked.

"My understanding is that living a life where one does not repent from the life of sin will not allow a person to inherit the kingdom of God. I don't believe that we have a black and white rule as to whether a person who commits suicide will go to heaven or not. It depends on the life that person has lived and whether he has accepted Jesus as his personal Savior and lived according to His principles."

"So Porchia, you are saying it depends on how Big John lived his life, not the way he ended his life," I said.

"I am saying it is between God and that person, and neither you nor I can judge. I just hope that Big John established his relationship with God and that he will inherit the kingdom. I know that he had a good heart. But I also know that having a good heart is not enough."

"I just don't understand why Big John did not trust in the Lord. As Aunt Hattie would say, 'I will trust in the Lord until I die'," I said.

"Yes, God wants us to have faith in Him. Taking your own life begs the question of whether or not you have faith in Him. However, as Christians, we all falter in our faith at times, but this does not necessarily prevent us from entering the kingdom of heaven. But a continued pattern of not having faith in God means that you don't have a real relationship with him."

I didn't know if I felt better or worse after speaking to Porchia. I just wished I knew how Big John was feeling before his death so we could have gotten him the help he needed. We treated his physical body, but ignored his mental and spiritual well-being. I knew that I would have to help Sweezy get through this difficult time. He had no one else in this life but me. I know that Big John asked Sweezy to take care of me, but I felt that I would need to take care of him.

Chapter 32

Porchia, Sweezy, Big John's ashes, and I flew to Las Vegas. We arrived at the hotel where I had made reservations, and they said that they did not have a reservation or any rooms available. The only hotel we could find was the Four Seasons and they only had a Presidential Suite available. Porchia was a little disappointed that she could not get her own room, but the suite was large enough for four adults to live in comfortably. We were particularly impressed with the floor to ceiling panoramic view of the Strip, especially at night.

Sweezy was hell-bent on having our ceremony at the same chapel where Michael Jordan and Juanita married. I agreed, but demanded a drive-thru wedding at the Little White Chapel. There were cars lined up for the drive-up ceremony. Porchia, our one and only witness, laughed the entire time, saying that this was the cheesiest thing that we could ever have done. Instead of allowing the chapel to take pictures, we took selfies to capture memories of our wedding day. We spent our honeymoon night going to the Michael Jackson show and watching Sweezy play craps at various casinos. Las Vegas, the hotel, the strip and the ceremony were not the highlights of my trip. I was just so happy to become Mrs. Sylvester Stone, and nothing else mattered.

We stayed two nights in our presidential suite before heading to the Grand Canyon to scatter Big John's ashes. Sweezy told me we were taking a small plane, but I did not expect the plane to be able to carry only four passengers. I prayed the entire trip because we must have hit every bump there was in the sky. One time I thought we had come to the end of our lives because the plane dipped about five feet.

I was so happy when we landed. I thanked the pilot several times for flying us safely to the Grand Canyon. I immediately began begging Sweezy to forego the little plane ride back and drive us back to Vegas. Sweezy stepped away to speak to our pilot. When he returned to us, Sweezy looked back at the pilot and said, "We will see you in about an hour or so."

We carried Big John's ashes with us on the Grand Canyon Skywalk. We walked to an area where there were limited people. Porchia said a prayer, Sweezy said a few words to Big John, and I sang "Missing You". We all held the urn and allowed the ashes to flow just as our tears were flowing. We stood there for a while until Sweezy said, "Let's go."

I did not want to press Sweezy about finding a rental car, so I just followed whatever he was going to do without asking questions. When we made it back to the airfield, there was a limousine waiting for us.

Sweezy looked at me and said, "You and Porchia go get in the limo and I will go settle our bill with the pilot."

My heart smiled knowing that my husband recognized my fear, and without my knowledge, made certain I had nothing to fear.

When we reached the limousine, it was filled with snacks, water, sparkling cider, and champagne. When Sweezy got into the limousine, he tuned into the satellite radio so we could listen to contemporary jazz. Sweezy led a toast to Big John. Oh, how I wished I could have had just one glass of bubbly! But I toasted with my glass of sparkling cider. We ate and drank until we reached Vegas. By the time we reached Vegas, Sweezy was drunk, Porchia was lit, and I was sober and mad about it.

Our plane left early the next morning so we decided to go back to the suite. Once there, we were exhausted so we ended up crashing for the night. Before drifting to sleep, I remembered that we had not had sex since we married. I attempted to wake Sweezy up so we could consummate our marriage, but my husband would not move. He was knocked out.

When we arrived back in Houston, Porchia began packing for Durham. It was difficult watching her get her things together to leave Houston. I felt that our time was very much limited because she also spent time with Tracy and her other siblings. She was also hanging out with Pastor Sadiq a lot. Porchia still insisted that they were only friends.

We all gathered at the house prior to her departure to have a going-away party for Porchia. I wished that I could have been happy for Porchia and her journey, but I felt myself moping most of the night, wishing that somehow I could keep her near me a little longer. Sweezy must have been reading my emotions because he kept hugging me all night and telling me that everything would be okay.

I had not moved any of my things to Sweezy's house because I wanted to remain home until Porchia left. Sweezy caught me in my bedroom sitting on the bed.

"Queen, I have an idea. Why don't we change our reservations to leave on the same day that Porchia leaves to go to North Carolina?"

"I guess."

"What's wrong?"

"I'm missing her already. We have lost so much this year. I hope I don't lose her."

"She is just going away to school. You are not losing her."

"But this is the first time that we will be apart."

"I remember a time that you two would have done anything to be apart," Sweezy said, laughing.

"No, that was Porchia! I never wanted to be apart from her."

"Well, I think it would be a great idea for all of us to leave at the same time."

"I am sure you are right. We just need to be certain the clubs are okay before we leave."

"I have been wanting to speak with you about that," said Sweezy.

"Can we talk about that later? I want to talk with Porchia."

"Are you coming home tonight?" Sweezy asked.

"No. I want to stay here until Porchia leaves. Will you stay with me?"

"Yeah, no problem. I need to let Ms. Marvelle know that we won't be home tonight."

Once everybody departed and Porchia went to her room, I knocked on her door.

"Come in," Porchia screamed.

I walked in and she was packing. She asked in a cheery voice, "Hi, Mystery, what's up?"

"I just wanted to check with you and make certain you were okay, whether you needed anything?"

"No, I am good. I am not traveling with much. I decided to have my luggage delivered."

"Are you ready to do this?" I asked.

"Do what, Mystery?"

"Start your new life," I responded.

"I don't know if I am so much starting a new life as just entering a new phase. And I am excited about this phase."

"Well, I don't know how I am going to do without you," I said.

"I will visit and you will visit. You are still planning on staying with me while you open the North Carolina club, right?"

"Yes. But it will not be the same. We have always been together since your birth, Porchia. I know that you did not know that I was your mother, but in my heart, you were always my daughter. So many times I wanted to tell you that I was your mother, but I was afraid of the DuBois Curse."

"The DuBois Curse? What are you talking about?" asked Porchia.

"I thought all of the women in our family were cursed to be whores. And I said I would do anything and everything in my power to make certain that you were not a whore. Part of doing everything in my power included not letting you know the line of descendants that you came from. So many times I wanted to tell you, but I thought I would be letting the Curse win."

"Mystery, I don't believe in curses, but I believe that you and Aunt Hattie did a great job in raising me. I look back and remember how I treated you and I feel badly about it. You single-handedly took care of a household on your own. Who does that these days? So you have no reason to apologize. You did whatever you could to make certain that I had opportunities that I might not otherwise have had. Instead of holding your head down, you should be raising your head up. Sweezy calls you Queen, and you are deserving of that title."

By this time, I was so emotional I could not hold back my tears. I said, "Porchia, that is one of the kindest things I have ever heard from you. Thank you."

Porchia came over and hugged me and said, "No. Thank you!"

After we finished bonding, I told her that Sweezy and I would be leaving when she left so she could ride to the airport with us. She told me that Pastor Sadiq had volunteered to take her and that she preferred this because it would be too emotional seeing me and Sweezy when she left. I was disappointed, but I knew that we both probably would have an emotional public breakdown so I told her I understood.

I went to the room and found Sweezy fast asleep, fully clothed across my bed. I realized it would be difficult for me to leave the room that I had for almost thirty years. Porchia was not the only one starting a new life. I started feeling nostalgic and decided to go into Aunt Hattie's room. I had a conversation with Aunt Hattie.

"Aunt Hattie, I don't know what I am doing and I am scared. You were here to guide me through this life's journey. Porchia has grown to be such a lovely young lady, but I am not ready to let her go. It seems like just the other day I was holding her in my arms, and now she is leaving me forever. I know that this is part of life and that she would not be with me forever. But this feeling is the most difficult thing I have ever experienced. I don't know how I will make it without her. How I wish I could turn back the hands of time. I know that I have a new life ahead of me, a new husband, a new baby, but I don't feel that I am ready. I need to know that you are still with me."

I immediately felt a cold wind rush through the room followed by a comforting feeling. I laughed and said, "Okay, Aunt Hattie, I know you are still with me. Can you let God know that I will need Him to guide me and help me through this phase of my life? As you often said, 'Can't nobody do you like Jesus'. Well, I need Him now and forever."

I sat for a while on Aunt Hattie's bed and the door slowly opened. I was relieved when I saw that it was Porchia. She came over and sat next to me and said, "Okay, Mystery, it is my turn to spend time with Aunt Hattie."

I laughed, kissed her forehead, and left the room. I knew that she probably would stay the night in the room, which she did often after Aunt Hattie's death. After saying goodnight to Porchia and closing Aunt Hattie's door, I felt a renewed confidence that everything would be well.

Chapter 33

I cleaned up my room at Aunt Hattie's and moved most of my things to Sweezy's. Sweezy noticed that I called the house his and he asked me what he had to do so I could think of the house as ours. I told him that I would be okay, it would just take time.

Ms. Marvelle was so sweet and she did everything to make me comfortable. She consulted with me about everything from the meals to the housekeeping. I was a little concerned about living with a woman that I did not know, but we bonded quickly. It was as if she had always been part of my life.

****

We left for our honeymoon the same day that Porchia left for school. Bora Bora was exactly what Sweezy and I needed. We stayed in our hut over the water for seven days. We periodically went out for lunch. Most of our dinners were served in our hut. We talked, laughed, and made love most of the time. Sweezy was a little concerned about us having sex and I had to explain to him that I was only six weeks pregnant, and there was nothing he could do to hurt the baby. I told him that the baby would be hurt if we did not make love. That was all that my husband needed to hear because he made love more passionately than he ever had before. I remember when Emmit would take me physically to another world. Sweezy took me physically and mentally to another world. I wish I could have just frozen time and remained in this space forever. The only thing missing was Porchia.

When we arrived back in Houston, we both hit the ground running. Sweezy traveled to Austin and Dallas while I went to North Carolina to check on Porchia and our business venture.

Porchia seemed to be fitting into her new environment well. Between classes, we would take time to go shopping and dining. I was also trying to make sure that I kept fit for me and the baby, so I continued to exercise and drag Porchia with me. She seemed to not be engaging in as much exercise since she started school. The best part of staying with Porchia was the discussions we had about God and spirituality. She gave me more insight that I ever had. I remembered a while back the scripture that Chardonnay gave me in relation to forgiveness and trespasses. I asked Porchia what trespass meant in the biblical context.

Porchia said, "Trespass means harm done toward you."

For some reason, I had always remembered the scripture so I asked Porchia her interpretation of Matthew 6:14-15.

"Well, Mystery, this is basically a sermon given by Jesus called the Sermon on the Mount. Jesus is speaking about principles that Christians should follow. This particular reference deals with forgiveness. It tells us that we must forgive as God forgive us and it gives us the specific consequences of not forgiving, which would be that God would not hear our prayers. In fact, by not forgiving, we are blocking any blessings that He may have in store for us."

"Well, when I read it literally, it seems to say that even if I am saved, but don't forgive, I won't be forgiven by God; therefore, I can't be saved. Is that what you understand from that scripture?" I asked.

"I am still learning and I have a lot more to learn. Anytime I read the scriptures, I pray and ask God to help me understand. I have read Ephesians 2:18 that speaks to how we are saved. I understand that this scripture says that we are saved by the grace of God and through faith, not through anything that we have done," said Porchia.

"Porchia, but I still don't understand whether a person who does not forgive will get to the kingdom?"

"The act of forgiving is something that God has told us to do, but it does not save us. Our faith is what saves us. But one who believes in God and has faith in Him will follow His Word, which includes love and forgiveness. I know there are a lot of people professing Christianity, but not embracing the values of Christianity. Therefore, I would question whether a person who goes around with an unforgiving heart has accepted Jesus."

"You seem to be focused on the relationship with Jesus," I said.

"It is all about the relationship and following the footprint that Jesus laid when He walked this earth. Okay, Mystery, why all of the questions about forgiveness? Is there something I should know?"

"There are some things that I wonder about and thought I could talk about it with my intelligent, theological school-attending daughter."

Porchia laughed and said, "As I tell everyone, God is not through with me yet."

When I left, I felt a lot better about the distance between me and Porchia. I realized that we would always be attached no matter what the distance.

I was so happy to see Sweezy when I got home and it seemed like he was even happier to see me. He picked me up off my feet and swung me around for what seemed like five minutes. I was dizzy by the time he let me go.

I asked, "Did you miss me, or did you feel like exercising?"

"Both. How was your visit with Porchia?" Sweezy asked.

"Amazing!"

"And how is our business venture going?"

"Not as good. I think I really need to spend more time there."

"You want to leave me?"

"No. I want us to get a place there."

"Mystery, remember when I said we need to talk?"

"No, but what's up?

"I have been thinking about getting out of the business, especially now with you having a child. We really don't need the money. Between our assets, Big John's, and my investments, we don't have to work a day more in our lives. We can dedicate our time to us, Porchia, and our baby. I just want for us to enjoy each other, take vacations, and just live the life that God has blessed us with."

"Wow! I don't know if I can do that. I have worked since I was thirteen years old."

"I have worked since I was ten, so I understand. But why do this when we don't have to do it? The money we could get from selling our places would also set our kids up for whatever they need. I have already been approached by an investment group that is very much interested in purchasing all of our entertainment businesses."

"Sweezy, I don't know."

"Please, Queen, just think about it. Remember how much fun we had in Puerto Vallarta? Every day should be like that. I am tired of hustling and really have no reason to continue the hustle."

I told Sweezy I would think about it, but there was no way I could not do something to keep me busy. I knew the baby could keep me busy for at least five years, but what would happen after he or she entered school? Plus, I enjoyed what I did and could not imagine leaving the business forever.

Since Sweezy asked me about selling, it seemed like problems popped up in Dallas, Houston, and Atlanta at the same time. He handled issues in Dallas and Houston while I told him I would travel to Atlanta and stop in North Carolina. I wanted to take every opportunity to see Porchia whenever I could. I spent three non-stop days troubleshooting our issues in Atlanta, and by the time I got to North Carolina, I was exhausted. I had hired a manager to oversee the remodeling of our North Carolina site, but it seemed like we had very different ideas.

I realized then that I probably should just plan on spending a few weeks in North Carolina because I would not be up to running back and forth. Before leaving, I told Porchia I would be back the following week and probably stay for about two weeks. Porchia was excited about me staying with her for a while, but I was not certain Sweezy would be so happy since he was trying to get me to slow down.

My flight from Durham to Houston was a little taxing on me. Sweezy picked me up at the airport and when he saw me, he told me I look exhausted. He made the decision that he would take me home so I could rest for the day. I had several appointments that I had to make the following day so I did not argue with him.

When we arrived home, I took a shower and collapsed. Ms. Marvelle attempted to wake me up for dinner and I told her I was too tired to eat. My stomach started cramping so I got up to use the bathroom. When I went to the bathroom, I noticed that I had passed some blood. I read somewhere that is was normal to spot during your first trimester. I took a note to tell my obstetrician during my next visit.

The last thing I had to do before leaving for North Carolina was get my hair done and go to my doctor's appointment. I did not like going to the beauty shop with a crowd of people so Shayla, my hairdresser, regularly made me 9:00 a.m. appointments. I asked if we could move it up an hour because I had a 9:00 doctor's appointment. I had been going to Shayla for at least ten years, so she would adjust her schedule to accommodate me. I walked out of the beauty salon feeling better than I had in a while.

I arrived to my doctor's appointment a little early. The receptionist told me that Dr. Joseph would be with me shortly. Dr. Joseph was one of the best African American female OB/GYN doctors in the country. She had a full load of patients and was not accepting any new patients, but I knew her brother so I had contacted him to see what he could do.

He personally asked her to take me in as her patient. She initially refused and wanted her partner to see me, but somehow he convinced her to take me. I was grateful for all of the contacts I had made over the years and the extent to which people would go out to assist me. I guess God had been good to me. As Aunt Hattie would say, "God is better to you than you can be to yourself."

Dr. Joseph came into the patient exam room with her normal smile and perkiness and asked, "Well, how are my favorite patients

, Mrs. Dubois-Stone and her little one doing today?"

"I am feeling better than I have felt in a long time, Doc. I had been experiencing severe nausea and cramping, but I am feeling a lot better now," I responded.

"Any vaginal bleeding?" she asked.

"Yes, once. But about two days after that I began feeling better and no more discharge."

Dr. Joseph looked at me and said, "Mystery, I would like to do an ultrasound."

"Sure, doctor. Will I be able to see the baby?"

"Well, at your stage we would normally be able to see the gestational sac. A few weeks later you would be able to see the embryo. I am going to do a transvaginal ultrasound, which will allow me to get a better pic of the sac."

She performed the ultrasound, which was a little uncomfortable. She then told me that she needed to draw some blood. Then she asked me when I had passed blood. I told her it was three days ago. She told me to take it easy and that I would be hearing back from her soon. The way she looked at me, I knew something was wrong.

I asked, "Is everything okay?"

She responded, "Don't worry. I just need to confirm some things."

"Doctor, I was planning on going to North Carolina for two weeks. Would that be okay?"

"I will know after I get back the results. I will call you later on this afternoon."

"Now you have me worried, Doctor."

"Don't worry. Everything will be okay."

Chapter 34

I got dressed, feeling very uncomfortable about my visit. I could not wait until I received a call from Dr. Joseph. I was walking out of the hospital when I saw one of the girls that used to work at The Club. She greeted me with a hug and smile.

"So I heard you were getting married."

I held my hand up, smiled, and said, "I done it, girl!"

She laughed and said, "Congratulations."

"So what are you doing here?" I asked.

She responded, "You remember Chardonnay?"

I thought to myself, *I would like to forget her.* I responded, "Of course I remember Chardonnay."

"Well, Chardonnay is in the hospital. She has been diagnosed with leukemia and will die if she does not get a donor."

"What!"

"Yeah, she looks really bad!"

"What type of donor does she need?"

"A bone marrow is what they call it. I was tested, but I was not a match. Chardonnay has really changed her life around. She would do anything for anyone that she could. I once saw her take off her sweater to give it to a homeless person. I don't understand why things like this happen to good people."

"I am sorry to hear that too. Well, it was so nice seeing you, Chilly. You look good, girl. I hate that I have to run, but I have another appointment," I said.

I pretended I was going to my car, but when she was out of sight, I went back into the hospital. I asked for Chardonnay Henry's room. Once I found it, I looked in and she was laying there almost lifeless. I stepped quietly into the room and she looked over and smiled. I did not know what to say, so I said, "Girl, why are you in that bed?"

"Hi, Mystery. It is so nice of you to come by and see me."

"I just found out that you were here."

"I never expected to be here, but it happened. I am learning that tomorrow is not promised so we should make the best of today."

"Stop talking like that. You have a long life ahead of you."

"I am trying to face reality. The doctors are being honest. They have given me approximately a month to live."

"Well, the doctors are probably good but they are not God. How did you know that you were sick?"

"It came on all of a sudden. My body and joints started aching. I was always so tired. Then I could not hold food down anymore until I eventually lost my appetite. After drastically losing weight, I decided to go to the doctor. They ran tests and that is when I found out I had leukemia."

"I am so sorry, Chardonnay."

"Why are you sorry? You had nothing to do with it."

"I just am. Well, I have another appointment, but I will be back to see you."

"I don't want you to come because you feel sorry for me."

"I will come because I want to, not because I feel sorry for you."

"Thanks, Mystery. But you owe me nothing."

I thought about my conversation with Porchia about forgiveness and I responded, "Nothing but forgiveness. I never forgave you for what you had done in the past. But I want to let you know that I forgive you."

"That means a lot to me. Thanks for coming by,"

"You hang in there and I will see you soon."

I left her room and went to the nurse's station to find out about how I could be tested to see if I could possibly be a match for my sister. The nurse put me in touch with the lab, and I went down there right away. I had to complete a questionnaire that asked a million questions. A nurse reviewed my answers and she told me I did not qualify to be tested because I was pregnant. She informed me that pregnant women could not be bone marrow donors.

I left the hospital worried about Chardonnay. She laid there looking so helpless. For the first time, I wanted an opportunity to get to know her. Maybe someone would be a donor match for her. I went home and Sweezy was not there yet. I started packing for North Carolina with Chardonnay on my mind. My phone rang and it was the doctor's office.

"May I speak to Mystery DuBois?" said the voice on the other line.

"This is she."

"Could you hold on for Dr. Joseph please?

"Sure," I responded.

I waited for about thirty seconds before anyone came back on the line.

"Hi, Mystery, this is Dr. Joseph."

"Yes, Doc. Is there a problem?"

"I would normally ask you to come into the office, but I know that you were expecting a call from me today," said Dr. Joseph.

"Yes."

"I am sorry to inform you that you had a miscarriage."

I did not know how to respond or what to say. I was in shock.

"Mystery, are you there?"

"Yes, Doctor."

"Are you okay?"

"No, Doctor, I am not."

I ended the call and just sat on the bed in a catatonic state until Sweezy came home.

Sweezy immediately recognized something was wrong. "Queen, what's wrong?"

I could not answer.

He bent down in front of me and asked, "Queen, are you okay?"

All I could do was shake my head from side to side. I tried to speak, but nothing would come out.

"Mystery, you have me worried. Please speak to me."

All I could do was stare. I had no energy to speak.

Sweezy grabbed me and said, "Baby, come on. Please let me know what is going on."

I whispered, "I need to lay down."

He took off my shoes and laid me down. He then got a blanket to put across me while I laid on the bed. I must have laid there for hours with my eyes open and my brain shut. I could hear him having conversations with people, but I could not understand what was being said. He would periodically ask me whether I was okay. I would shake my head. I felt that if I spoke, I would explode. I eventually dozed off. I woke up and Sweezy had my head in his lap, playing with my hair.

I sat straight up and said, "I lost the baby."

He looked at me and said, "Yes, I know. Dr. Joseph called and I spoke with her."

"Why did this happen to us, Sweezy?"

"I don't know, Queen. But I have learned that our plans are not necessarily God's plans."

"Are you okay with us losing our baby because it was not in God's plan?" I asked.

"No, but I have to believe that He is the man with the plan," Sweezy said.

"It does not matter to you because you did not want the baby anyway!" I screamed.

"Stop it! You know I was just as excited as you about us having a baby."

"Oh, you don't remember running out when I first told you the news?" I asked.

"That was just a knee-jerk reaction. I came to my senses. This hurts me as much as it hurts you. Queen, we will get through this together."

"I don't know Sweezy. I have been through a lot. But this hurts a lot."

"I will make certain that we get through this. I am your husband and I am here to take care of you and make you smile as much as possible."

"I just want to curl up in a ball and die."

"So you would bail out on me and Porchia? I have news for you: I refuse to lose another person I love. So if I have to spend the rest of my life making you want to live, that is what I will do!"

Chapter 35

I was in bed for three days until Porchia showed up one day, yelling at me to get out of bed.

She stood over the bed and said, "Look, I am missing classes because you have decided to give up on life. This is not you, Mystery. You are a fighter. You still have a lot to do and a lot to live for. You are going to get out of bed and get cleaned up. This room stinks!"

"Porchia, go back to school and leave me alone."

"I will leave you alone once you get yourself back together. And if you don't get up soon, I will just stay here forever."

That girl was talking stupid! She knew she had to get back to school and her life. She probably did not think I could ride her out. But I am just as stubborn as she is. I raised myself up and said, "Get comfortable, because I am not going anywhere." Then I lay back down and covered my head with my pillow, just wishing she would go away.

After two days of Porchia pounding me every minute, I gave up, got up, and showered. She insisted that we go out to eat at Pappadeaux's and insisted that I drink a Category Five. I actually ended up having three Category Fives and life did not look as so gloomy as it had for the last week.

I actually laughed at some of the stories that Porchia shared with me over our dinner. She had an odd way of seeing things, and I loved viewing life through her lens. She asked me whether I would go back with her to North Carolina. I told her that I needed to take care of things at home. As soon as I had things stable, I would go spend time with her. How could I forget that I already had such a beautiful daughter that still needed me? There was no way I could give up on life now.

Porchia had a date with Pastor Sadiq while I set up a date with my doting husband. He had been by my side, with me stinking and all, the whole time until Porchia arrived. I think he knew exactly what I needed to get me going. We rented a limo and went out club-hopping around H-Town. I had not had this much fun in a long time. It was funny because I used to know all of the latest dances. I found myself asking some of the younger girls to teach me the new line dances. Sweezy sat back and smiled the entire night. After the last club, we went to the Port of Houston and made out like teenagers. Then we asked the chauffeur to take us on a ride along the Loop. Sweezy and I made out in the limousine while driving around the 610.

Things were almost getting back to normal when Porchia left for Durham. I was back in the saddle assisting Sweezy with our businesses. Sweezy and I decided that we would not rush into having kids. I was surprised when he said he would be fine with just the three of us: me, him and Porchia. I told him that I would not be satisfied, and I thought that we should work on having another child in another year or so. We agreed to table the discussion until a later date. I made an appointment with Dr. Joseph to get a check-up to see if there was some reason I could not carry a baby. I had not had a discussion about why I miscarried.

When I arrived at the hospital, I thought about Chardonnay. I decided that after my appointment, I would check to see if I was a match to be a donor for Chardonnay. Dr. Joseph ran tests and told me that based on her experience; she thought it was a chromosome problem with the baby. I seemed to be healthy enough to have a viable, full-term pregnancy. She warned me that when couples are anxious about having a baby, it makes it more difficult to conceive. She told me we should just enjoy each other and we could probably be pregnant in no time. This was good news to me, but I knew that Sweezy was in no rush.

I decided to go visit Chardonnay after being tested. The lab told me someone would be in touch with me if I was a match. Chardonnay looked worse than when I last saw her. She could barely speak, but she tried to smile for me. I never noticed how beautiful she was. Even sick, she was lovely. Her eyes smiled at me the entire time. I sat there and held her hand and told her she did not have to say anything. I just wanted to come by and spend some time with her.

As I was talking to her, James Henry, Chardonnay's dad, walked in. I had to take a double look because he was fine. I guess my mom always had good-looking guys because Duke was a nice-looking man too. James Henry commented on how Chardonnay and I had a strong resemblance to each other and he could definitely tell that we were related. After exchanging a few pleasantries with him, I looked at Chardonnay and told her I would be back to visit her soon.

She smiled and let out a weak, "Thank you."

After leaving the hospital, I thought about the wasted years. If I would have known, I could have developed a relationship with my sister. I never even had a close girlfriend, so this would have been a welcome change. So much had been lost over the last year. As Chardonnay said the last time I visited her, tomorrow is not promised, so we need to make the best of this day.

I immediately called Sweezy just to tell him that I loved him. He asked me if I was okay and I assured him that I was. I then called Porchia, but it went to her voicemail. I left her a message that I loved her. She called me back five minutes later asking me whether I was okay or not. After hanging up with Porchia, I committed myself to telling the people that I love that I loved them often.

The hospital contacted to tell me that I was indeed a match. Now I would have the difficult task of telling Sweezy about my decision. I told Ms. Marvelle to make him some curry goat so I could break the news about what I was going to do for Chardonnay. When he sat down to the table and saw the goat and a bottle of his favorite cognac, Remy Martin Cognac Black Pearl Louis XIII, he looked at me and said, "Mystery, I thought we agreed to ice the baby thang for a while."

"Love, this is not about a baby. I wanted to have your favorite things here because you have been so good to me."

"Looks like you trying to get me drunk. I ain't doing no drunk in love."

"Sweezy, relax. I ain't trying to get what is between your legs right now."

"Okay, tell me what is going on."

"Let's finish eating and we will talk," I said.

"Talk now so I can enjoy my goat without trippin' about what you got under your sleeves."

"Sometimes you can be impossible."

"And sometimes you can be sneaky. Talk, woman."

"Oh, I done gone from 'Queen' to 'woman'?"

"You will always be my queen, woman," he said, laughing. "But you need to let me know what's going on."

"I am going to be a donor for Chardonnay."

"What? What are you donating?"

"My eggs, since you don't want me to use them before I lose them!"

"Are you serious?"

"No, I am doing a bone marrow transplant."

"Okay, how serious is that?"

"I was hoping you come with me to the hospital when they explain it. Chardonnay looks like she is getting worse. So hopefully we can do it right away."

"Are you sure about this? Are there any risks to you?"

"Very limited risks. I think most of the risks involve going under general anesthesia."

"No matter how good you think the deed is, I don't like the idea of anything that may be a risk to you."

"Sweezy, I need you to support me in this. I am going to do it. I would love my husband to be there in a positive manner."

"I will definitely go with you to the hospital."

After scheduling the bone marrow transplant, Sweezy must have called Porchia to give her all the details. Porchia called me and told me what a selfless act I was doing for Chardonnay, and how proud she was of me. I still had not shared with Porchia everything that Chardonnay had done in the past, but I knew in my heart it was the right thing to do. After all, Chardonnay was blood.

Porchia told me that she was coming down for the procedure, but I told her not to come. I told Porchia that the procedure would take only a couple of hours and there was a possibility of me being released that day. Porchia insisted that if I did not allow her to come, she wanted her representative, Pastor Sadiq, there during the procedure. I agreed, thinking that it would not hurt to have a man of God on our side.

Chapter 36

I woke up in more pain than I had ever felt. My first thought was, "God, I have forgiven her, but I will never forget this pain I am feeling for her." When I looked up, I saw Sweezy, Porchia, and Pastor Sadiq.

I looked at Porchia and asked, "Why is your head so hard?"

She responded, "I got it from my mama."

I tried to laugh, but it hurt like hell.

Sweezy bent down to kiss me and asked, "How are you feeling, Queen?"

I looked at him and said, "I can't answer that question truthfully because a minister is in the room."

Pastor Sadiq replied, "Mystery, I am praying for your speedy recovery. Please know that you can always be yourself around me. I may be a minister, but I am human."

The doctor came in and said, "Hi. I see you finally decided to wake up. You had some good sleep, young lady. I will need to check you over." He looked at Sweezy, Porchia, and Pastor Sadiq and asked them if they would mind waiting outside.

Sweezy looked at the doctor and said, "Yes, I mind. I want to be here with my wife."

"Sure. If that is okay with the patient," the doctor responded.

"Please, Doctor. He will start a riot if he does not stay," I said.

Sweezy had that "you dayum right I will" look on his face.

After the doctor examined me, I asked how Chardonnay was doing.

"Chardonnay is recovering well," the doctor said.

"Well, can I visit her?"

"As soon as you are cleared."

"What's wrong? I thought I would be able to leave when I came out of the anesthesia."

"You are running a slight temperature. I want you monitored overnight."

Sweezy looked at the doctor and asked, "Is that common?"

"Well, patients have different reactions. I suspect that her temperature will be normal by morning. I just want to monitor her to make certain everything is okay."

Sweezy looked worried so I did not want to ask the doctor about the unbearable pain I was feeling in my back.

But the doctor must have been reading my mind because before leaving he said, "Mystery, I know that you are probably in a lot of pain right now, but we will be administering pain medication and something to bring down your temperature. You should be feeling better in about seven days. I won't be in tomorrow, but Dr. Gentry will be checking in on you. I have already passed your information on to him and I will update your file. But if you have any questions for me, you can always call." He then handed me a card and said, "You have given your sister the wonderful gift of an extended life. That was a very compassionate act."

Sweezy thanked the doctor and I just laid there thinking about life. In an instant, people you love can be taken away.

After the doctor left, Sweezy said, "A penny for your thoughts."

I responded, "I am just so happy to be around people I love and people who love me back."

"Where did that come from, Queen?"

"I don't know. Sometimes we don't count our blessings, and I want to make sure I do that more often. More than anything, I want to see Chardonnay as soon as possible."

Porchia came back into the room without Pastor Sadiq and I looked at her and said, "I love you."

She looked confused and said, "Yeah, I know, and I love you too."

Sweezy looked at Porchia and said, "Yeah, she is trippin'. It must be the drugs."

"No! I just want the people that I love to know that I love them," I said.

Porchia looked at me and said, "Well, I just came back from visiting Chardonnay."

"How is she?" I asked.

"She seems to be doing okay, but she is very tired. They made me put on a protective suit, with a hat and a mask. I wonder what all of that is about."

"Did you ask?" I said.

"No, I didn't."

"I am sure it is just to protect her," Sweezy said.

"Yeah, probably," said Porchia.

"Porchia, when are you going back to school?" I asked.

"As soon as you are released and okay."

"I wish for once you would just do what I asked. I asked you not to come."

"I wanted not only to be here for you, Mystery, but also for Chardonnay. I have been talking with her a lot over the last month."

"About what?" I asked.

"About a lot of different things. She has grown spiritually over the last year, and we have had a lot of discussions about God."

I started feeling jealous over Porchia having a relationship with Chardonnay. I could not help but think how I had to share Porchia with Aunt Hattie. I did not want to share my time with Porchia with anyone else. I knew in my heart that this was selfish, but I could not help feeling that way.

"Well, that is good. I hope you have helped her with her spiritual growth, 'cause God knows she needs it," I said.

Porchia answered, "Yes, we are all in need of spiritual growth. Each day we live, we should be growing closer in our relationship with God."

"Porchia is right, Queen. And you probably should rest."

I knew this was Sweezy's way of shutting me down. I gave him a sharp look and said, "I feel fine."

Porchia said, "I guess that is my cue to leave." She came over and gave me a kiss and said, "I will see you tomorrow."

"Okay, sweetheart. Be careful," I responded.

After Porchia left, Sweezy looked at me and said, "So you were about to rehash the past after giving Chardonnay blood so that she could live?"

"I don't know why. I got jealous when Porchia said she was talking with Chardonnay."

"So you can talk to Chardonnay, but Porchia can't?" Sweezy asked.

"I know it does not make sense. But I guess I am being just overly protective."

"No. I think you are being overly selfish," Sweezy said.

"You want to start a fight with me about being selfish when I am the one lying in this bed in pain after saving Chardonnay's life!"

"Yes, and the next minute you are upset because she is trying to have a relationship with her niece," said Sweezy.

"I don't want to talk with you about this. I need to rest."

271

"I am staying here with you tonight," Sweezy said.

"No. Go home. I will rest better if I know you are comfortable," I said.

"Well, I will rest better if I am with you," Sweezy said.

I did not argue because I wanted him to stay. The bottom line was that I would have been upset if he did not stay.

Chapter 37

I have experienced that time heals all wounds. I was feeling a lot better within two weeks after the bone marrow transplant to Chardonnay. Chardonnay was feeling better within two months after the transplant. She was released from the hospital within three months of having the transplant. During her hospital stay, Chardonnay and I developed a relationship better than I thought was ever possible.

Upon her release from the hospital, Chardonnay did not have a place to live because she did not have a job. Porchia and I decided it would be a good idea to let her stay in my old room at Aunt Hattie's. Although Aunt Hattie was long gone and the house legally belonged to Porchia, we both referred to the house as Aunt Hattie's.

As time passed, Chardonnay and I spent a lot of time together and once she completely recovered, she started managing Aunt Hattie's Retreat in Houston. It allowed me more time to concentrate on North Carolina and Atlanta, while Sweezy had oversight of Dallas and Austin. Although I was ambitious and desired to open venues in other cities, Sweezy shut down all of my ideas. He told me we were on a five year retirement plan.

As part of our five year retirement plan, Sweezy and I decided that we would grant one-half ownership of Aunt Hattie's Retreat in Houston to Chardonnay, if she agreed to be the sole managing partner. We then would sell our four remaining venues. This was our compromise because I told Sweezy I could not allow Aunt Hattie's Retreat go into the hands of someone that was not family.

In a million years, I could not have hand-crafted a better husband than Sweezy. I remembered when I used to look at him and I thought that he was nothing but a street thug. He might still be considered a street thug by some, but he took care of family, home, and business. He did not let anything affect his ability to take care of what he called his. If I kept it real, I knew that I could be difficult and that I had selfish ways at times, but he always treated me with patience, respect, honor, and dignity - even when I didn't deserve it. Although we often debated whether we would have kids, I knew that he would also make a great father. I knew that my husband wanted to make me happy and that I would eventually win this argument.

Porchia was excelling at Duke Divinity School while working a full-time job and keeping a relationship alive with Pastor Sadiq, who was also pastoring and working on his Ph.D. They seemed to have a perfect long distance relationship. He visited her as often as his schedule allowed, and she did the same thing in return.

Porchia had a way of making everyone feel as if they were the most important person in her life.

I was not sure how she did everything that she did, but Porchia flourished into the most loving, beautiful, talented, dedicated, spiritual, young black woman I had ever met. She wrote several books on theology and was featured as one of the most prominent young black theologians in *Essence*. I knew that her road was not always easy, but I was so proud of her accomplishments, and the fact that together, we had defeated the DuBois Curse.

Faking the Dream

Stayed tuned for JJV: The Storyteller's third book, *Faking the Dream*. This book gives insight into Tyrese Gamble (Ty) who is a NBA star that is torn between his sexuality and the woman he really loved. Ty went from rags to riches once he signed his contract with the NBA, but still was not living the dream. Ty was caught in a world between gay and straight and hated the world that he felt he was forced to live. He knew that the NBA would frown on his sexuality if he confessed to anything other than being a card-carrying heterosexual. Therefore, he spent most of his life pretending that everything was good, that is, until he met Porchia Williams. She was everything he ever wanted and needed in a woman, but rejected him once she discovered him having sex with a teammate. He would spend the rest of his life trying to get her back because she was the only remaining catalyst to him living the dream. Until he won over her heart again, he would spend his life faking the dream.

www.ingramcontent.com/pod-product-compliance
Lightning Source LLC
Chambersburg PA
CBHW051247260626
47162CB00002B/655